"I wonde... through your mind," Lucas said lazily

Anet froze, then produced a smile. "I was thinking that willpower—determination—is an important quality."

He watched her with brilliant, half-closed eyes. "Very. Of course, too much—or wrongly directed—and it can be dangerous."

"So can anything," she retorted.

Leaning back in his chair, he asked dryly, "Compassion?"

"If it becomes overprotective and debilitating."

"You're a hard woman." A smile failed to take the sting from the words.

"Possibly." She wasn't going to let him get away with that. "Any emotion or attribute can become dangerous if it's allowed free rein. Even too much common sense can deprive a life of excitement and joy."

"So you don't believe in allowing a grand passion free rein?"

She hesitated, conscious that beneath the amused tone and light mockery there was something else. "No," she said cautiously.

Olivia Nicholls and the two half sisters Anet and Jan Carruthers are all born survivors—but, so far, unlucky in love. Things change, however, when an eighteenth-century miniature portrait of a beautiful and mysterious young woman passes into each of their hands. It may be coincidence, it may not! The portrait is meant to be a charm to bring love to the lives of those who possess it—but there is one condition:

> *I found Love as you'll find yours,*
> *and trust it will be true,*
> *This Portrait is a fated charm*
> *To speed your Love to you.*
>
> *But if you be not Fortune's Fool*
> *Once your heart's Desire is nigh,*
> *Pass on my likeness as Cupid's Tool*
> *Or your Love will fade and die.*

Meant to Marry is Anet's story and the second title in Robyn Donald's captivating new trilogy THE MARRIAGE MAKER. Look out next month for Jan's story in *The Final Proposal*, which concludes the trilogy and solves the mystery of the haunting image in the portrait.

Books by Robyn Donald

HARLEQUIN PRESENTS
1783—PRINCE OF LIES
1794—INDISCRETIONS
1803—ELEMENT OF RISK
1865—THE MIRROR BRIDE

ROBYN DONALD

Meant to Marry

Harlequin Books

TORONTO • NEW YORK • LONDON
AMSTERDAM • PARIS • SYDNEY • HAMBURG
STOCKHOLM • ATHENS • TOKYO • MILAN
MADRID • WARSAW • BUDAPEST • AUCKLAND

ISBN 0-373-11871-6

MEANT TO MARRY

First North American Publication 1997.

Copyright © 1996 by Robyn Donald.

Printed in U.S.A.

CHAPTER ONE

'AND who,' Georgia Sanderson purred to her companion, 'do you think this is?'

Anet Carruthers turned slightly. The newcomer was haloed by a dazzle of sunlight so that all she could see was his outline, but that was enough to sharpen the strange apprehension that troubled her as he strode along the dock towards them. Anet was accustomed to being the tallest person around, and her astonished glance told her that this man towered over her by at least four inches and, like her, was big-boned and strong.

Her gaze slid helplessly to an extremely handsome face, its autocratic framework revealing an authority and control she could only envy. Big as he was, he didn't carry an ounce of excess weight. Wide shoulders narrowed to lean hips and long, heavily muscled legs. And in spite of his size there was nothing ponderous about him; he walked with the smooth, athletic grace of a supremely fit man.

Although Anet immediately turned back to the tourist group on the diving vessel, she was left with an impression of inborn mastery, of a dominance that was both uncompromising and dangerously compelling.

Trust Georgia to notice him first. Anet's sister Jan, who moved in the same circles in Auckland as the beautiful redhead, said that Georgia's antennae were always at the ready for a good-looking man. It was not a compliment. Jan and Georgia did not like each other. Now Anet noticed the woman's green eyes darken with alert anticipation as the tip of her tongue flicked across her full mouth, moistening its already lustrous sheen.

Not just Georgia either! Every other woman on board watched the man on the wharf with the same intent, intrigued awareness, paying involuntary female homage to his unforced masculinity.

Lord, Anet thought with edgy exasperation, he must be sending off pheromones like nobody's business. Thank heavens she didn't go in for all that man-woman stuff!

Pitching her voice to be heard above the soft wash of the waves against the dock, the bustle of the wharf and the ever-present sigh of the trade winds that cooled the South Pacific island of Fala'isi, she went into her spiel.

'Before we leave the dock,' she said, smiling with what she hoped was a confident, professional charm, 'do check to make sure every exposed inch of skin is slathered in waterproof sunscreen. Ears can get burnt very badly, and so can ankles and the insides of your knees—even the soles of your feet.'

Her gaze lingered a moment on Georgia. Scott, bless his generous heart, had responded to the other woman's impudent use of Jan's name with an offer of a free morning's diving for her and her friend. Irritated, Anet had had to stand silently by and endure Georgia's sly, satisfied smile.

'I'm already wearing sunscreen,' Georgia said, dragging her eyes away from the approaching man to reject Anet's unspoken comment with a haughty stare.

There was no tell-tale gleam on that silken, pale skin.

Stifling her exasperation, Anet returned, 'Not enough, I'm sorry. Fala'isi is well within the tropics. The sun here is even fiercer than it is in New Zealand. It can really fry your skin, so I'm going to insist that you all put extra on, and I'm afraid that every two hours I'll act like a schoolteacher until you do it again.'

The curvy little redhead pouted, her bright eyes disparaging as she scanned Anet. 'I'll be careful,' she protested. 'I'll stay under cover when I'm not diving.'

Anet had been well briefed. 'The sun's rays bounce off the surface of the sea,' she said, trying to soften her answer with a smile. 'In fact, even wearing clothes you're not entirely safe. UV rays can penetrate cloth—especially pale material. We can't take responsibility for you unless you apply sunscreen.'

'I have—'

A darkly masculine voice interrupted, 'She's right, you know. The tropical sun is cruel to people who don't take it seriously.'

Uttered with cool authority, in the sort of tone that commanded instant respect, those few words lifted the hairs on the back of Anet's neck. Automatically she glanced over her shoulder.

The man from the wharf now stood a few feet behind her, his narrowed gaze fixed on Georgia. Beneath thick black lashes his eyes gleamed turquoise, almost pure blue with just enough green to issue a challenge. But then his whole face dared you not to respond to its lean, ruthless good looks.

A sudden chill in Anet's stomach expanded to a wintry emptiness. Struck by an intense and frightening foreboding that this man was going to have an impact on her life, she turned away, swallowed and said woodenly, 'You heard the man, folks. He's right, so slather on the stuff—and be generous.'

At that moment Scott came bounding up from his devotions over the engine. 'Hi, Lucas,' he said, beaming, although clearly surprised. 'What are you doing here? No, don't tell me now; I haven't got time. Do you want to come out this morning?'

'If you'll have me,' the stranger said. His New Zealand accent was barely noticeable, lost in the voice that proclaimed an assurance so deep-rooted it was probably encoded in his genes.

Anet, who had had to work very hard for her confidence, subdued a prickle of animosity.

Sure enough, Scott laughed. 'There's always room for you, you know that.' He turned to Anet. 'Everyone here?'

Trying to ignore the man whose presence she could feel, watchful, unmoving, almost elemental behind her,

Anet said neutrally, 'As soon as they've all put on their sunscreen we'll be ready to go.'

Resigning herself to the inevitable, Georgia gave a slight, elegant shrug that spurned the bottle Anet proffered, and fished her own expensive brand from her smart bag. When a covert glance revealed that it was over SPF 15, Anet relaxed. The last thing she wanted was a parboiled tourist. Scott's wife Serena, whose place she was taking on the diving vessel, had warned her that some people just wouldn't accept how severe sunburn could be until they'd experienced the heat and intensity of the tropical sun.

'And it is *not* good for business to dry-fry the customers,' she'd said wryly. 'You have to be tough, Annie; some of them are total idiots and will do everything they can to avoid putting it on.'

Like the beautiful Georgia, who was now applying lotion with a sinuous languor that made an erotic exercise of the business—an exercise revealing the many and varied charms of her slender body. Her absorption, her refusal to look once at the man who stood just behind Anet, made it more than obvious at whom she was aiming the whole little production.

It should have been amusing, perhaps rather—pathetic? It was not; in fact, it took all of Anet's control to quell the sudden, sickening resentment that assailed her. She found herself understanding why her sister found Georgia so irritating.

'Right,' she said briskly when at last every revealed inch of the redhead's honey-smooth skin had had cream smoothed into it with slow, sensual strokes, 'we're ready.'

And that was when Georgia stretched, only to slip as the boat lurched in the wash of one of the bigger tourist launches which had just taken off.

With a gasping, choked yelp she went over—fortunately on the lagoon side, not against the heavy, unforgiving piles of the wharf.

'Look out!' someone yelled in panicky, high-pitched tones.

Anet fixed her eyes on the cloud of brilliant red hair that bobbed up once before sinking too far down. Slim, pale arms flailed above the surface then disappeared. Without further thought Anet dived overboard, hoping, as the warm waters of the harbour closed around her like a benediction, that the woman was a better swimmer than she appeared to be.

And that the large, laden tourist launch stayed well out of the way.

Several strokes of her powerful arms took her to the floundering tourist, once more on the surface. One look at her face, distorted with genuine fear, convinced Anet that she was going to have to use a release hold. As soon as she got close enough she lifted her arm into the air.

When Georgia grabbed desperately at it with both hands 'Anet wrenched it down, and used the other woman's brief confusion to hook her under the chin and kick strongly back towards the boat.

They were almost there when Georgia spluttered furiously, 'All *right*. You can let me go now.'

Well, Anet thought wryly, Jan had stated often enough that what few manners Georgia possessed were invariably used as weapons; even allowing for the shock of that sudden immersion, it seemed Jan was right.

Anet released her, but shepherded her back to the diving platform at the stern of the boat. It had happened so quickly that Scott hadn't yet got there; waiting for them instead was the big man who had, Anet was sure, inadvertently caused Georgia to lose her balance.

Anet could feel frustration and anger emanate from the elegant redhead. No doubt she felt she'd made a fool of herself. Then, so quickly that Anet gave a startled look ahead, the other woman's resentment evaporated, her frown replaced by a faint, smug smile. Lucas Whatever-his-name-was was crouching on the dive platform, and, although Scott had arrived by the time they reached the boat, it was Lucas's outstretched hand that Georgia grasped.

A powerful heave brought her up and into his arms, where she clung, shivering artistically. Against his lithe leanness she looked very small and fragile. Scott hovered, talking very fast, ignored by the other two.

Anet pulled herself onto the platform and stood upright, feeling her eyes widen beneath lowered lashes as she watched Lucas soothe the woman.

Lord, she thought hollowly, no wonder Georgia had lost her footing. He was gorgeous—like something out of a virgin's fevered dreams of romance. That perfectly proportioned body was balanced by a face that could sink a thousand hearts. Not that he projected the sullen sultriness of a male model, with an appeal owing more to fashion than to aesthetics; this man's beauty was elemental, the result of commanding bone structure backed by a potent, hard-honed magnetism.

And she, Anet realised grimly, was no more immune to that overwhelming combination of dangerous good looks and virile male authority than the woman in his embrace.

At that moment his head came up as swiftly as a predator scenting prey. When her glance met enigmatic turquoise eyes her pulse quickened, and a shuddery little chill tightened her skin.

All sensible thoughts stumbled to a halt; running a hand through her short black hair, she gave him a weak smile. His brows straightened, but then Scott, who apparently belonged to the school which believed that to be effective an apology should be repeated a hundred times, started again, and Lucas looked down again at Georgia, breaking off that moment of silent, almost subliminal communication with a merciless lack of interest.

'I'm terribly sorry,' Scott babbled. '*Terribly* sorry. That should never have happened—'

'It's perfectly all right,' Georgia interrupted graciously, smiling. 'I'll be fine as soon as I'm dry.'

Furious with herself, Anet jerked open a locker and got a towel, offering it to her. It was greeted with a dubious frown.

'I have one of my own, thank you,' Georgia said, looking past Lucas's broad shoulder to her slightly less glamorous friend, who, with eyes fixed on Lucas's face, held out a bag.

Reluctantly, the redhead stepped away from Lucas and drew out a hotel towel, saying to Scott, 'It was my fault— I just slipped when that other boat went past us. So clumsy.' Looking at Anet, she finished sweetly, 'Don't tell Jan, will you, or I'll never hear the last of it. Thank you for coming for me—I'm really quite a good swimmer, but you were certainly quick off the mark.'

Clever, Anet thought judiciously. In two sentences she'd managed to imply both that Jan was a harridan and that any fool should have seen that she was capable of saving herself—and her last comment had hinted at a certain surprise that someone as big as Anet could move fast. Probably she had hoped that Lucas would rescue her!

She should, Anet thought sourly, have let her thrash around until she'd exhausted herself. Hoping that her guileless smile would at least prick the other woman's armour of self-assurance, Anet ran the rejected towel over her own fine hair, pushing the soot-coloured salty strands back off her face.

'All part of the service,' she said lightly.

After an uneasy glance Scott interposed, 'If you want to change there's a cabin below that's—'

Switching a thousand-watt smile onto him, Georgia said blithely, 'Oh, I don't think so, thanks.' And with an arch look at Anet she finished, 'I'll dry myself down and put some more sunscreen on, though.'

Forbearing to point out that the stuff she'd applied was waterproof, Anet said with serene good humour, 'An excellent idea.'

'Oh, yes, you mustn't get sunburned.' Tenderly, Scott escorted the other woman into the shade cast by the canopy.

Anet stood back, but Lucas waited for her to go ahead of him, his cold, beautiful eyes narrowed and intent. The salt water stains made on his cotton shirt and trousers by Georgia's body were already drying quickly in the sun.

As Anet made her way towards the bow she thought she felt that steady, strangely inimical gaze right through to her bones, and chided herself for her stupidity.

Scott caught up with her almost immediately, accompanied by the newcomer.

'Annie, this is Lucas Tremaine,' Scott said enthusiastically. 'Lucas, this is my cousin, Annie Carruthers, who's helping me out for a while. Lucas sailed his yacht down from Hawaii last year, Annie, then left it at the marina here when he had to go to New Zealand.'

'How do you do?' As she held out her hand Anet produced the right sort of smile—pleasantly impersonal. And was appalled at her swift, rapidly suppressed thought. Why am I not five foot three and curvy and redheaded, instead of six feet tall with more muscles than your average prizefighter? Why can't I show off in a bikini that makes me look like a seductive bird of paradise?

Shamefully ridiculous questions! Long before she'd left high school she'd come to terms with her Amazonian build.

Lucas Tremaine's hand was bigger than her long-fingered one, and certainly much stronger. Over the years Anet had been faced with quite a few men compelled by ego and insecurity to prove their power to a woman almost their size, but although this man's grip was firm he made no attempt to wring her fingers off.

'I thought your name was Anet,' he said, his eyes lingering on her wet T-shirt.

She wondered whether she had seaweed in some strategic place and looked down, but it was still pristine white, with the logo of Scott's company gleaming across her breasts. And beneath it her decent blue swimsuit prevented any sort of exposure. Withdrawing her hand, she shrugged. 'My family call me Annie.'

'A very mundane name for an unusual woman. I watched you win your gold medal at the Olympic Games,' he said, those brilliant eyes strangely oblique. 'I thought you looked like Atalanta.'

She had long ago forced herself grimly past that memory. 'Atalanta was a sprinter,' she said with a light lack of emphasis.

His mouth tilted into a smile. 'Of course. Like an Amazon, then—or better still Hera in majesty.'

Surely he was taunting her? However, her startled glance discerned nothing in his expression but an aloof self-possession. She smiled. 'I rather like that image,' she said, 'although the mind boggles at the thought of the queen of the gods in a tracksuit.'

'I imagine she'd have found one very useful,' he said gravely. 'Why did you drop out of sight so quickly?'

Although there was no blatant curiosity in the deep, intriguing voice, Anet chose her words carefully. 'All I ever wanted to do was win an Olympic gold. Once I'd accomplished that I had other things to do.'

'Annie's just finished training as a physiotherapist,' Scott said proudly. 'She's damned good. She got my shoulder going really well.' He flexed it experimentally. 'Yep, just like new. What are you doing here, Lucas? Are you planning to sail off into the unknown again? Not in the hurricane season, surely?'

Before Lucas could answer either of his questions a flash of movement from one of the paying clients recalled Scott to his surroundings. 'Hell—we'll talk later,

OK? I'd better get this show on the road before someone reminds me we're supposed to be diving.'

He disappeared to the wheelhouse. Feeling obscurely tentative, Anet nodded at Lucas Tremaine and said, 'If you'll excuse me, I have to let go forward...'

'I'll do the aft line,' he said.

At her doubtful look his wide, hard mouth lifted in a fascinating crooked smile. 'I've spent most of the last five years at sea,' he said gently, and went through the crowd of tourists like—like a hot knife through butter, she thought, half amused, half bewildered.

Whatever charisma was, he possessed it—and the kind of self-assurance that came close to arrogance. It didn't seem fair that as well as size and looks and presence he had, if the clothes and watch he wore indicated anything, a substantial bank balance. A darling of the gods, she thought ironically.

Hera in majesty! Really!

Scott's voice broke into her thoughts. 'Ready?'

Embarrassed, she hastened up to the bow, thankful that there was no one around to see the rush of colour to her skin.

Today, besides the well-being that came from fitness and health, something else ran through every cell in Anet's body—a kind of primitive excitement she ascribed to the sheer delight of being alive in the sultry golden heat of a tropical morning, with the scent of coconut and frangipani and salt in her nostrils and the sunlight glittering and dancing over a sea as brightly coloured and much more transparent than Lucas Tremaine's eyes.

And where, she wondered, grabbing the heavy loop of rope from the islander who slung it down into her hands, had she heard that name before? If he'd been an athlete she'd have remembered him. He wasn't the sort of man you forgot. Not if you were a woman anyway.

She squinted down at the stern. Yes, he knew exactly what to do. The group of divers stayed respectfully away

from him while he dropped the rope loop into its place
and straightened to fend the boat off from the piles. Beneath the cotton shirt, muscles moved across his back
and down his arms. Something tightened inside her;
hastily she transferred her gaze across to the white line
of the reef.

The engine increased its noise as they swung away from
the wharf. Lucas stepped back into the cockpit and
smiled down at one of the women. Anet reminded herself
that she had to entertain this group until they reached
the coral gardens where they'd anchor to dive.

Back in the cockpit, she picked up the microphone
and began to expound on the sights as Scott headed the
craft towards the gap in the reef formed by the flow of
fresh water from the river.

Ahead was a busy day. They'd dive, then call in at
one of the small motu—the Polynesian word for island—
on the reef, where they'd eat a barbecue beneath the
coconut palms. After that this group would be brought
back to the town to be replaced by a load of snorkellers
who didn't want to venture beyond the silken aquamarine waters of the lagoon.

She was glad she'd been able to answer Scott's call
for help three weeks ago. Although she found some
tourists rude, and others foolish, most were very
pleasant. And she loved Fala'isi. The island, its green
mountain spine and lush vegetation forming a beautiful
backdrop to the sea and the blindingly white beaches,
epitomised the South Sea paradise embedded so deeply
into the fantasy life of those who lived in colder climates. Scott was her favourite cousin, and the social life
was fun too—a vigorous mixture of expatriates, locals
and tourists.

All in all, she thought, looking across the glinting
waters of the lagoon, life probably couldn't be more
perfect.

The cool, challenging speculation in a man's sea-blue
gaze meant nothing.

Although she did her best to keep her eyes off Lucas Tremaine, she noticed when Georgia approached him and engaged him in conversation, her sparkling eyes and tempting little smiles making her interest only too obvious.

It should have been amusing to watch her hastily hidden pique as first one, then another woman drifted across, eager to join in the conversation, yet an ignoble pang of envy shot through Anet.

And that's enough of that, she told herself sternly. You've accepted that you're never going to know the easy, casual interest these women feel, or their confidence. Experience had taught her that her height, combined with the powerful build of an ex-javelin-thrower, was not alluring.

No man ever saw Anet Carruthers as sexy; likeable, certainly—almost one of the boys—but not feminine, not the sort of woman who could drive a man mad. Even the man she had been engaged to, the man who'd dumped her for a slim, small woman barely reaching her shoulder, had *liked* her.

Mark had worried about hurting her, but he hadn't thought her capable of intense emotional distress. Of course, she thought aridly, turning her head to point out the position of a famous shipwreck, he'd been right.

Although she'd been hurt, she hadn't been shattered. She must have missed out on the capacity to lose herself in love as other women seemed able to do. Even her unrequited love—and she had loved him—for Drake Arundell when she was eighteen hadn't blighted her life.

She'd recovered with astonishing speed, although Drake was still her ideal of what a man should be like. Which might, she thought, eyeing Lucas Tremaine covertly, be the reason this man made strange things happen to the base of her spine. He and Drake were alike, both big men, but there was more to their similarity than the physical; both possessed an air of controlled power.

Anyway, she was now in full command of her life, looking forward to a happy and useful future.

'Great view,' an amiable masculine voice said.

It belonged to an amiable masculine face. Supporting herself against the side of the boat, Anet smiled at him. 'Isn't it just?' she said. 'What more could anyone want? Glorious weather and the prospect of a day spent diving and eating, then lolling the afternoon away on a coral beach—'

'Heavily anointed with sunscreen,' he interpolated, his brown eyes laughing.

Her eyes gleamed with answering amusement. 'Of course,' she said solemnly.

'And you forgot something in your catalogue of pleasures.'

'Oh, a hundred things. Fala'isi is full of delights.' Sunlight soaked through her, drying out the material of her T-shirt and bathing suit, melting down to her bones.

'Well, this is important. Good company.'

She looked around the boat, feeling a bit sorry for him. Lucas Tremaine seemed to have snaffled all the available women. As her gaze passed over the cluster of them about him her mouth curved sardonically. He looked up, and for a moment she had the giddy and entirely erroneous idea that they duelled across the distance.

'Well,' she said vaguely, looking unseeingly at the man beside her, 'every pleasure is intensified by good company.'

A wave sloshed across the bow, sending a glittering, evanescent veil of spray into the air. Warned by the sprinkle of drops across her face, Anet flicked on the microphone again. 'We're approaching the gap in the reef and it looks as though it could be a bit bumpy today, so hang on everyone. If you don't like getting damp, it might pay to take shelter.'

A few seconds later the first comber caught them. Although Scott knew the opening as well as any islander, and was ready for it, a gurgle of laughter whipped Anet's head around. Her mouth compressed. Georgia was once more snuggled against Lucas Tremaine, her sleek, pale body a blatant contrast to his golden tan and corded muscles.

An odd little quiver wrenched Anet as Lucas set the woman on her feet, smiling down at her while he said something that brought a slow, sleepy smile in response.

Immediately he stepped back, made a further comment that tilted Georgia's lushly blooming mouth into more laughter, and left her, heading towards Anet.

He was the most handsome man she had ever seen— as beautiful as a god. And as dangerous, instinct warned her; the magnificent combination of form and face was almost overshadowed by the aura of authority and power that he radiated.

As he came towards her the smile he'd bestowed on Georgia faded. Anet was accustomed to being sought out—many New Zealanders knew who she was, and quite a few people liked to talk to someone who had won a gold medal for New Zealand at the Olympics—so there was absolutely no reason for her stomach to clench and her palms to sweat.

'Is he a friend of yours?' the man beside her asked casually.

'Of Scott's,' Anet responded absently, then, aware that she was being rude, smiled at him. 'Scott owns the boat.'

He had good manners. When it became obvious that Lucas Tremaine intended to speak to her he said easily, 'I'll see you later, then.'

She gave him her best smile. 'You will,' she told him, and kept that smile pinned to her face as he moved off and Lucas arrived.

'How long is it before we get there?' he asked.

She looked along the reef. 'About twenty minutes.'

'Where's Serena?'

'In Australia. Melbourne, actually. Her mother's in hospital for tests.'

'I'm sorry to hear that. How is she?'

Anet bit her lip. 'Not too good, unfortunately. Serena rang last night; Scott says she's worried. The tests were positive, and her mother has to have an operation.'

'That's tough,' he said, frowning. 'Lucky for them both that Scott managed to find someone to take her place so quickly.'

Although his skin was glossed by sunscreen, he was tanned a deep gold that indicated long hours of exposure to the elements. When she looked more closely she could see tiny lines at the corners of his eyes.

'I was the logical person to ask. I have a diving instructor's certificate and I was at a loose end. The clinic I was to start work at burned down,' she explained. 'It will be a couple of months before it's rebuilt, and in the meantime the owner's working from home. He didn't have room for me, so when Scott sent out his SOS I was able to come up.'

'As I said, lucky man.'

Watching her cousin at the wheel, she said drily, 'Oh, he'd have found someone, but he might have lost a few days' work.'

'I gather he isn't qualified to take out divers?'

'Not yet. He and several men from the local family he's in partnership with are sitting for the instructor's certificate now, but none of them have got it yet. They're doing the boatmaster's too. In Fala'isi you have to have certificated people on each boat before the local tourist board will let you take divers out. I can understand that, but when you think that the Polynesians have been sailing around the Pacific for the last three thousand years or so, making them take the boatmaster's seems like overkill.'

'Ah, but tourists need special treatment,' he said a little mockingly.

He was right, of course. The subject seemed to have reached a dead end, so after a moment of searching for a new topic she ventured, 'Scott said something about your yacht. Are you planning to sail somewhere?'

'No,' he said, adding with an edge to his voice, 'only fools go wandering around the tropics in the hurricane season.'

Absurdly relieved, she asked, 'Do you live on Fala'isi?'

'I've been living on the *Dawntreader* for the last few years, but I'm based in New Zealand now. I haven't had time to sail the *Dawntreader* there, so it's still moored in the marina here. Scott keeps an eye on it for me.'

She said wistfully, 'Sailing the Pacific sounds terribly romantic.'

'It can be.'

Something in his tone pulled the hairs on the back of her neck upright and then, too late, she remembered the reason his name had sounded vaguely familiar. 'Oh, yes, of course. I remember,' she said unevenly.

Lucas Tremaine had been an investigative journalist, a good one, working for a British newspaper when, in his early twenties, he'd been sent to cover an insurrection in San Rafael, a tiny Pacific nation. There he had met a young woman, married her and taken her to safety in England. But after his publication of several merciless articles on the abuse of power in her homeland, the house where he'd lived with his pregnant wife had been bombed. His wife had died in his arms.

After that he'd returned to San Rafael and disappeared into the jungle to join the freedom fighters in their bloody and merciless war. When at last they'd seized victory, he'd marched with them in triumph into the capital before disappearing into the solitudes of the Pacific Ocean on his yacht to write a book about the experience.

As though driven, he'd followed that one with others—books that dealt with dangerous and hidden facts. He had untangled the roots of piracy in the China Sea and had written about the sex trade in Thailand and the slavery that ensued from it.

Each book had caused a considerable scandal; each had been a bestseller. And each had made him powerful enemies.

Anet looked at the hard, inexorable face, and her blood ran cold.

'It's over,' he said quietly.

But nothing like that was ever over. Oh, the grief faded, and eventually you learned to live with the memories, but they were always there. Eight years after her grandmother's death, she still missed her.

'So what are you doing on Fala'isi?' she asked, aware that the change of subject was awkwardly abrupt but unable to think of another way of getting past the sticky patch. Jan, or their mother, would have known exactly how to deal with the situation her clumsiness had caused, without compounding the pain.

But then Jan would never have blundered like that.

'I came to see you,' he told her, measuring her reaction with a speculative gaze.

Anet's eyes widened. The subtly mocking smile on his beautiful mouth was matched by a glimmer in the sea-blue eyes; both set warning bells ringing.

'Why?' she said briskly, curbing the unfounded excitement that tightened her nerves. Although he wasn't intruding on her personal space, he seemed too close.

'Olivia Arundell sent me,' he said. 'Apparently it's your birthday today.'

Astonishment rippled through her voice. 'Well—yes.'

'Your twenty-fifth birthday.'

'How did you know?'

'Olivia told me. She also sent you a present.'

Years before, when Drake Arundell had married Olivia, Anet had thought her heart would break; only willpower and stubbornness had pulled her through. Yet it had been impossible to resist Olivia, who had become a close friend.

'Did she?' Anet said, thinking that it was just like Olivia to do something so unexpected. 'Isn't she a darling! Did you tell her you were coming here?'

'No,' he said calmly. 'I was on my way to Hawaii when she asked me if I'd mind stopping off and giving it to you.'

Anet couldn't help her incredulous laughter. Her eyes flew to his, found them cool and intent and alarmingly disturbing. Impossible to guess what he was thinking. '*Olivia* did?'

His mouth quirked. 'Somehow it's difficult to say no to Olivia Arundell,' he drawled.

Well, yes, but still... A sideways glance convinced her that this man would say no to anyone if he felt like it. So why was he here? 'You mean she asked you to break your journey just to deliver a gift?'

'I gather it's an important one.'

'We only give each other tiny presents,' she said.

'This is no bigger than the palm of my hand.'

Intrigued, she responded, 'It seems an odd thing for her to do, but I suppose she must have had a reason for it.'

'I'm sure she did.'

A note in his voice drew her eyes swiftly upward. There was something intimidating about the gleam in his impenetrable eyes as they met hers, lingered for a moment, then drifted down her face to come to rest on her lips.

Instantly they felt hot, and twice as large as normal. With an acid distaste out of all proportion to the discovery, she realised that he was one of those men who flirted automatically with every woman, young or old, who came their way. She'd heard it referred to as 'charm', that intensity of interest—for as long as they talked to you they made you feel that you were the most fascinating person in the world.

Anet didn't consider it charming, and had learned not to take anything such people said or did at face value. It was a trick—part of a cynical armoury.

So she forced a guarded smile and said, 'Well, it was lovely of her, and thank you so much for bringing it to me.'

'Your mother and sister—Jan, is it?—were there too,' he said. 'They sent messages to you.'

'They fussed, you mean,' she guessed, holding back a groan. Presents from her family had arrived a couple of days ago, complete with instructions from her mother on how to avoid sunstroke and food poisoning. It was a wonder Jan hadn't added her bit—she usually found something to warn her about.

'Somebody did say something about taking your vitamin pills,' he agreed solemnly.

Although Anet was accustomed to her mother's and her half-sister's constant concern, it was embarrassing to be told of it by Lucas Tremaine. Hoping it didn't sound artificial, she produced a laugh. 'I'm twice the size of both of them,' she said, 'but they still don't think I can be trusted to look after myself when I'm on holiday.'

He held her gaze for a few unsettling moments, but all he said was, 'Holiday?' Dark brows raised, he looked at the fifteen divers who were beginning to point and exclaim as they neared the coral gardens. 'You call this a holiday?'

'Compared to the last few months it is definitely a holiday. I hope this unscheduled stop-over isn't making too much of a mess of your plans.'

'Not at all,' he said pleasantly. 'I might even decide to stay here after all. I've always liked Fala'isi.'

So there was no one waiting for him in Hawaii.

Quelling an unruly anticipation deep inside her, she said repressively, 'It's a very small place. Wouldn't you get bored?'

'I don't think so.' His lashes hid everything but a narrow sliver of intense colour. 'I could always settle down and grow cabbages.'

'Taro, surely, here?' The brittle note in her voice startled her.

'Whatever.'

'Wouldn't that be difficult? Once a wanderer always a wanderer,' she said, immediately irritated by the inane remark.

The chiselled line of his jaw hardened for a second, and the sculpted mouth thinned, but his eyes remained watchful and oddly enigmatic. 'Sooner or later even the most inveterate wanderer decides to settle down,' he said noncommittally.

'Excuse me.'

The peremptory note in the feminine voice grated on Anet's ear, but she turned instantly and smiled at Georgia Sanderson. 'Yes?'

'I'm thirsty,' the other woman said, disguising the sharp antagonism in her eyes with a flutter of lashes. 'You do have drinks, as the brochure said?'

'Yes, of course.' Only a few steps away behind a small bar in the cabin was Sule, eager to dispense drinks and snacks—as Anet had informed everyone over the microphone a few minutes after they'd left the wharf. 'I'll get you something now. What would you like?'

Georgia pouted for just long enough to show off her provocative lips. 'Something long and cold and wet— mineral water,' she said. 'I'm almost dehydrated in this heat.'

There was enough accusation in her tone to make Anet stiffen, but nothing showed in her expression as she said, 'Right, I'll be back in a moment.'

When she returned with a cold can Georgia thanked her prettily before, with a social ruthlessness that stunned Anet, dismissing her politely and firmly. Not that she'd have had a chance to continue talking to Lucas, for, as though the sight of the can had sharpened people's thirst, everyone wanted one.

By the time they'd all been served it was time to lay down the rules for safe diving. Georgia listened intently, although with the charming air of an adult humouring a child, as Anet took them through hand signals, the length of time they were allowed to stay under and the maximum depth.

It would, Anet thought wryly, be a long time before Georgia forgave her for that rescue.

CHAPTER TWO

WHEN the anchor rattled down Anet had the tanks checked for the final time and the divers organised into pairs. As Scott jumped into the dinghy to drop off the flagged buoy that warned of divers in the vicinity, she said to the group, 'I know you've already been asked this, but I have to tell you again that it is extremely dangerous to dive if you're at all prone to asthma—even if you only get wheezy when you have bronchitis.'

Everyone shook their heads solemnly. Anet couldn't stop herself from casting a swift glance at Georgia, and immediately felt ashamed. Irritating she might be, but it was clear from her familiarity with the gear that she had dived before.

'Keep checking your depth,' she continued. 'All the pretty fish and corals are close to the surface, so there's no reason to go below twenty metres. Once you do, the risk of narcosis increases significantly.'

Everyone nodded.

'If this is your first dive for some time you'll have got out of the habit of watching your gauges, so be vigilant.'

Everyone nodded again.

'All right, then,' she said cheerfully. 'In you go—and remember, no teasing the moray eels. They don't take kindly to it. And stay with your buddy. You are each other's safeguard.'

She noted their entry into the sea with an experienced eye. Yes, they all seemed to know exactly what they were doing—even Georgia. Either she'd been putting on a show back there in the harbour or she was one of those divers who used the buoyancy compensator as a back-up for their poor swimming skills.

Serena had warned her that occasionally you got some idiot who thought they didn't need instruction or training. People were strange. Why expose yourself to danger?

The approaching dinghy summoned her to the side of the launch. 'I'll stay out,' Scott called above the noise of the motor. 'You keep Lucas company on board, Annie. Ask Sule if she wants to come with me, will you?'

But Sule, tidying up at the bar before checking the till, hid a yawn behind an elegant hand and said, 'No, I'm going to have a sleep. My little sister was sick all night, so guess who didn't get any rest!'

When Anet relayed the answer Scott saluted and spun the dinghy, heading back towards the flagged buoy.

Skin prickling, very much aware of the man who stood beside her, Anet watched her cousin go, feeling as though she'd been deserted.

'You didn't have to stay to keep me company—you could have dived.' Lucas Tremaine's voice, deep, cool, with an intriguingly abrasive undernote, intruded into her thoughts.

Keeping her eyes on the strings of bubbles breaking on the surface, she replied, 'This lot are all competent in the water, so I don't need to get in with them. Besides, the water's so clear that if they stay close to the boat I can see them all from up on top. Which is where I'd better go right now.'

She turned and made her way to the top deck, both pleased and wary when he accompanied her.

'I presume they have to be competent to go down,' he said.

'Not necessarily. I can take beginners on a resort dive.'

'What's that?' He spoke absently, as though thinking of something else.

'They follow me around like ducklings after their mother while I show them the more accessible parts of the coral garden,' she told him, averting her eyes from the dark forearms on the guardrails. A panicky foreboding pressed down on her, drying her mouth, increasing her heart-rate as she fought to control it.

You're overreacting, she thought disgustedly, taking three deep breaths to calm her pulse. This man was no physical threat, and it was stupid to get into a tizz at the sight of his arms!

After clearing her throat she said, 'It's not diving as experts know it, but at least that way untrained swimmers get to see the fish and the corals.'

Her voice sounded perfectly normal, the words deliberate as they usually were, so why did she feel that she was gabbling? Leaning down, she pulled at one of the fenders to straighten it.

'Here, I'll do that,' Lucas said.

She turned her head, meeting his eyes with a tiny shock. 'I can manage.'

His smile was ironic. 'I'm sure you can manage almost anything you care to do,' he said, 'but give my shrivelled ego some consideration, please.'

She almost laughed aloud as he hauled the fender straight with a single smooth, effortless movement. Although some men took her height and strength to be a personal insult, she was prepared to bet a substantial amount that Lucas Tremaine wasn't one of them.

He coiled a loose rope with the careless skill of someone who had done the same thing hundreds of times. She asked, 'Are you working on a book now?'

'No.'

Not exactly communicative!

However, he went on easily as he came back to stand beside her, 'I've just posted a manuscript off.'

'So you're having a holiday?'

He flexed his hands on the guardrail, the long fingers curling around the warm wood, then relaxing. 'I'm researching the next one.'

'In Hawaii?' she asked faintly, wondering what on earth was dangerous enough to interest him there.

'Yes.'

'Have you ever thought of writing fiction?' She leaned out to follow the progress of a scarlet-bikinied diver.

He sent her a swift, speculative glance. 'Like many journalists, I've occasionally tossed around the idea of producing the next big blockbuster.'

It would be much less risky than gambling with his life, finding wrongs to be righted.

'I think you could do it,' she said, wondering at the anxiety that chilled her heart. 'You write very vividly. When will you know whether the one you've sent away has been accepted?'

'It was accepted before it was written.'

Her brows shot up. 'Is that normal?'

'I've got a good agent.'

Anet probably knew as much about the publishing world as he did about physiotherapy, but she was certain that it hadn't been his agent who had got his books accepted before they were written; his reputation must be excellent. And why not? She had read all of his books and found them utterly absorbing. Although he had glossed over the inherent perils of the research he'd done, each chilling, brilliantly written volume had read like a thriller—one with no happy ending.

He was easy to talk to, but then, she thought some time later, of course that would be part of his armoury of skills. As they kept a close eye on the divers in the coral garden he spoke freely of his life as a sail tramp. However, Anet noted, he mentioned neither his career as an investigative journalist nor his wife.

In return Anet told him about places she had been and the highs and lows and indignities of training to be a physiotherapist.

Later she would realise that she hadn't referred to her time as an Olympic athlete.

When the divers began to drift back to the boat Anet had to hide a little niggle of resentment. Lucas Tremaine was a fascinating man—dry-witted, none too acceptant of stupidity, and he could tell a story so that it interested you on several levels. And a man who just happened to look like something straight out of a fantasy, she reminded herself, watching Georgia dry herself down with maximum effect.

Anet counted all the divers off, then made sure they reapplied sunscreen. While Scott started the engine and headed the boat towards the little motu where they'd be having lunch she listened to excited comments about the marine life the divers had seen in the coral garden.

This was the part of the day Anet liked least. Usually somebody wanted to hear about her experiences as one of New Zealand's most visible sportswomen of a few years ago, and while she could understand their interest, it irritated her to be slotted into that mould for ever.

Well, there was one woman who wouldn't be interested in her athletic prowess, she thought with a hidden smile as Georgia preened herself in the sunlight.

Donning a hat woven skilfully from pandanus leaves, Anet helped Scott ferry people onto the hot white sand of the motu, where a barbecue had already been set up beneath a clump of coconut palms.

The two young men who barbecued the fish and chicken for their meal were from the same family group as Sule. Their tribal council and headman had set up a trust which partnered Scott and Serena and provided workers for the venture. The fish cooking on the coals— and the others that had been made into the dish known by so many different names across the Pacific, their succulent raw flesh whitened by the juice of local limes— had been caught off the reef only hours before by other members of the extended family.

Women of the village had made the salads in a brand-new industrial kitchen on the mainland and ferried them across to the motu in big insulated boxes. They had also set the table, twining crimson and gold hibiscus flowers with glossy green leaves across the stylised, elegant black and cream of the tapa cloth made to their own traditional design.

The motu, pretty as an emerald set in kingfisher-blue enamel, looked like a bright poster from a travel agency. And all to provide tourists with an exotic experience—one, Anet had quickly realised, they enjoyed very much.

'It's like paradise,' a big Australian man said now, gazing around at the glittering lagoon, the abrupt peaks in the centre of the main island, the graceful grey trunks of the coconut palms. He tried some of the fish salad and laughed. 'If my mother could see me now—she'd never believe that I ate raw fish and enjoyed it!'

'The lime juice actually cooks the flesh,' Anet said. 'Sort of, anyway.'

He grinned. 'I'm not going to tell her that. You're Anet Carruthers, aren't you?'

Schooling the resignation from her face, she nodded.

'I saw you at the Olympics,' he said. 'You were brilliant.'

'Thank you,' she said. At his next words she thought the air froze around them. His voice went on, but she couldn't hear what he was saying until she swallowed fiercely and cleared her ears.

'Whatever happened, you deserved that medal,' the man finished earnestly, the upward intonation of his voice at the end of the sentence revealing that, like so many others, he wondered whether perhaps she would tell him something no one else knew about the rumours that had shadowed her Olympic triumph.

The muscles in her face ached with the effort it took to keep them passive. Although it had happened years ago, the wound was still acutely tender—the only thing that would heal it would be Victoria Sutter's confession that she had lied.

And Anet knew just how likely that was.

She said calmly, 'Thank you.'

Lucas Tremaine's voice broke into the prison of her thoughts. 'Excuse me, Anet, but several people want to collect shells,' he said. 'Is it allowed?'

She met his assessing look with a feeble attempt at aplomb. Words stumbled from her tongue. 'I—yes, of course. Although they can't take any live shellfish.'

'You'd better show them how to tell whether they're alive or dead,' he said. When she didn't move he held out an imperative hand. 'Coming?'

Obediently she got up, gave the man beside her a vague smile and went with Lucas, mesmerised by his size, she supposed, or by the unfaltering strength she sensed in him.

'What's the matter?' he asked when they were out of earshot.

'Nothing.' The denial came automatically.

His brows rose. 'You went as white as a sheet, and although the insensitive clod you were with didn't seem to notice, you looked as though you'd been shown a glimpse into the pits of hell.'

Angered by his astuteness, she returned grittily, 'You should do well with fiction if you ever give it a try.'

He turned his head and looked her way. An inner chill shivered through her body; she had to grit her teeth to stop herself from flinching. Her chin came up as she stared back unwaveringly, defying him to comment.

Instantly it was gone, that secret, hidden menace, the cold power that had slipped its leash and blazed from his unreadable eyes for a fleeting moment before he'd reimposed control.

'Thank you,' he said ironically, and for the rest of the time they were on the island stayed close to her—like, she thought foolishly, a huge guard dog, more intimidating than he was handsome.

Back at Fala'isi he left them at the wharf, but before he went he found Anet and said, 'Scott says you're staying with him. How would it be if I drop the present around this evening just after seven?'

'Fine, thank you,' she said, fighting an odd mixture of anticipation and antagonism.

Time that afternoon seemed both to stretch to infinity and hurry past, so that when they arrived back at Scott and Serena's bungalow—set in suburbia that was familiar yet exotic, with streets shaded by coconut palms and scented by frangipani bushes, their cream and gold and cerise flowers uncurling from spiral buds between rosettes of large, lushly green leaves—Anet wondered where the hours had gone.

'I'm taking you out to dinner,' Scott said firmly as he switched off the engine of his somewhat aged car. 'And then we'll go on to a nightclub.'

'Dinner would be lovely, but I'm not a club person really, Scott,' she said quickly. Although the business was doing well, he couldn't afford to waste money.

'Come on,' he coaxed. 'I won't wear a T-shirt with "Paradise Diving" in big red letters all over it like I usually do, and I'll behave very nicely—no haring off to drum up clients, I promise.'

She gave him a teasing smile. 'You don't have to take me out, you know, even if it is my birthday. I'm perfectly happy staying at home.'

'I know,' he said earnestly, 'but bear with me, Annie. You've been a real brick, leaving everything to come up and help out, and I'd like to do something for you.'

'Well, I didn't get where I am today by refusing to go out with handsome men,' she said, smiling as she gave in. 'And you'd better wear that T-shirt—at least to the nightclub. Serena would never forgive me if you missed out on an opportunity to attract more customers. Where will we go for dinner?'

'I thought you might like to try the local Chinese restaurant. It's the best in the Pacific, and believe me, that means something, because there are some brilliant Chinese restaurants in the South Seas. Then we can go on to an island night in one of the hotels. It's always a good do.'

'What'll I wear?'

'Anything that isn't hot,' he said. 'Casual but pretty—that's what Serena calls the island look. Most of the women will probably be wearing sarongs.'

Anet regarded him with affectionate exasperation. Those sarongs would have been bought from hotel shops or the main street boutiques; they'd be expensive, the epitome of informal chic, and they didn't suit her.

'Casual but pretty I can manage, although it won't be a sarong,' she said, adding, 'Oh, by the way, Lucas is coming over at seven. He's bringing a present for me from Olivia and Drake Arundell.'

'Do you know him?' he asked. 'You didn't say.'

'No, I've never met him before, but obviously we share some friends. How did you get to know him?'

'I went to school with him,' he said. 'I was in his house when he was head prefect.'

Of course he'd been head prefect. 'What was he like?'

'Tough but fair,' Scott told her. 'Bloody clever. More respected than quite a few of the teachers.'

'Did you ever meet his wife?'

He whistled between his teeth. 'Yeah. Remember when Serena and I were in the Auckland-Suva yacht race? Well, he and Cara were in Fiji at the time. We saw quite a bit of them.'

I am *not* going to ask what she was like. To stop the impetuous words, she said remotely, 'That was a tragedy.'

Scott nodded, his cheerful face for once bleak. 'Yeah. She was— Oh, hell, every so often you meet a woman who really stands out, you know? Cara was beautiful, but she was open and easy, and funny with it, and somehow she made you feel that just to be alive was a wonderful thing. I couldn't believe it when I saw in the paper that she'd been murdered.'

'It must have been terrible for Lucas.'

'I don't know how he got over it. She doted on him, you could tell, and although he didn't show it so much, he thought she was everything. Hell of a thing to happen.

He's never said anything about it, but I think that's why he went bush after she died. He disappeared for nearly a year. Nobody knew where he was or what he was doing until he marched into the capital with the freedom fighters.'

'I suppose he blamed himself for his wife's death,' she said.

Scott nodded. 'Yeah. Years later in a bar in Greece I met a journalist who knew him quite well; he and I got talking one night over a bottle of whisky and he swore that Lucas had hunted down the men who'd planted the bomb.'

'Killed them?' she asked faintly.

'Well, delivered them to justice.'

Anet shivered. Yes, she thought. Yes, I can imagine him doing that. He'd be utterly merciless. 'Poor Lucas,' she said, unfolding herself from the front seat of the car. Poor Lucas, and poor Cara, and the poor unborn child.

Could anyone ever get over such wholesale destruction of their family?

If anyone could, Lucas Tremaine looked as though he was the man; he exuded a concentrated, self-sufficient toughness that had been grafted onto an already strong character. But even he might find it hard to forgive himself for the death of his wife.

'You have the shower first,' Scott said generously as they went into the house. 'I've got paperwork to do and people to telephone.'

Cool water washed away the sweat of the day, sleeking down her body, giving Anet an illusion of freshness as she shampooed. Once out, she dried herself off, sighed as the humid heat enveloped her once again and combed back her fine black hair, wondering just what Cara Tremaine had looked like.

Scott eyed her dubiously when she emerged from her bedroom. 'You should go and have a shopping session,' he said.

She knew what he meant. The linen shirt-dress, striped in off-white and a dusky pink, suited Auckland, not the vivid colours and heavy, sensuous atmosphere of Fala'isi. 'Perhaps I will,' she said airily.

He gave her a sharp look. 'Have you got any money? And don't frown—I know you. Too independent for your own good.'

She lifted haughty black brows at him. 'This sounds a little strange coming from the man who turned his back on his family to make his own way in the world.'

Grinning, he aimed a punch at her upper arm, then reeled back dramatically and shook his knuckles, wincing and blowing on them. 'God, will I never learn,' he mourned, 'that you've got muscles like a drain-digger?'

'If you keep punching me you'll learn it very soon.' She looked at him sideways and said demurely, 'Although you were never exactly noted for rapid understanding, were you?'

He opened his mouth to return her amiable insult with one of his own, then changed his mind. '*Did* you bring any money?' he persisted.

She sighed. 'We live in the era of the credit card, my dear.'

'Oh, yes, I keep forgetting you're an heiress.'

She said cheerfully, 'I used the last of Gran's money to buy into the practice.'

'So you've got—?'

She shook her head at him. 'Dad advanced me some money. I'm all right, Scott. I certainly don't need anything from you, and if by any chance I do, I'll let you know, don't worry.'

Scott's reply was forestalled by the sound of the doorbell. 'See that you do,' he said. 'That'll be Lucas,' and went off to let him in.

Anet smoothed a hand over her hip. Resisting the sudden need to swallow, she picked up a birthday card from a Canadian woman she'd beaten years before, after a particularly tense competition in Rome, and turned it over in her hands. In spite of their torrid struggle they'd become firm friends.

'Have a beer with us?' Scott was asking as the two men came into the room. 'Or better still, why don't you come out to dinner? We're going to The Jade Horse and then on to the Plaza's island night.'

An involuntary protest trembled for a second on Anet's tongue, before being swallowed unspoken.

'I didn't intend to butt in,' Lucas said, his expression unreadable. He wore grey trousers and a shirt that was superbly cut across his wide shoulders. Hair the golden brown of dark honey gleamed in the light of the central lamp; in his long, tanned hands he held a small package.

'You're not,' Scott told him. 'Is he, Annie?'

'No, of course not.' Smiling stiffly, she added, 'We'd like it very much if you came.'

He sent her a considering glance before saying with a politeness that came perilously close to parody, 'Thank you. I'd like it too.'

'OK, that's settled.' Scott grinned at them both and headed towards the door. 'I'll ring the restaurant.'

Anet put down the card and looked across at the man who stood watching her, his attitude oddly forbidding. Summoning a wry smile, she said, 'He feels he has to entertain me on my birthday.'

'You seem to be a close-knit family.'

'Very,' she said, thinking of her lovely, laughing mother and sister, and her reserved, drily humorous father, as well as his two sisters and three brothers— parents to a whole horde of cousins who had alternately delighted and plagued her childhood.

'You don't look much like your sister.'

'We're half-sisters, actually. Jan is five years older than I am.'

'Ah, that explains it. Here,' he said, proffering the parcel, 'is my commission.'

Anet took it and turned it over, more curious about Olivia's reasons for sending it with a courier than its contents. 'I wonder what it is?' she murmured.

He laughed softly. 'If you open it you might find out.'

So she sat down and, feeling absurdly self-conscious under his enigmatic gaze, began to take off the wrapping. Beneath it she discovered a flat box. After wrestling with the fastenings, and more bubble plastic than seemed necessary, she managed to get it open and slide its contents out. In her hand lay a tiny portrait in a frame. Anet gasped as she stared down at the delicate little countenance some eighteenth-century artist had painted on ivory.

Luminous, glowing, a very young woman looked out at the world with solemn blue eyes set in a sweetly imperious face. The features were fine yet not weak, and a squareness to the jaw hinted at an interesting personality.

'Intriguing presents you give one another.' Lucas's voice was noncommittal.

Her brows meeting, Anet looked at the back. A tiny clip held a flap in place. With extreme care she turned it over so that once more she could see the painted face. 'It's valuable, isn't it?'

'If it's genuine—and although I'm no expert it certainly looks that way—then yes, it's quite valuable. And very beautiful.'

It was obvious that he thought the second attribute more important than the first.

'There must be some mistake,' Anet said slowly. 'Olivia wouldn't give me anything like this. It looks like a family heirloom.'

'She told me to look after it and said you'd probably protest but to ignore you. She means you to have it.'

The young woman gazed serenely back at Anet. 'Her expression seems to change,' she said, before she realised how stupid such a remark was.

'May I have a look?' Lucas asked, and came over to sit beside her.

Silently she handed the portrait to him, watching as the lean fingers deftly took the dainty thing. Her stomach jumped.

'I wonder who painted it,' he said. 'He was a master, whoever he was.'

She said, 'It could have been a woman.'

'Do you think so?' The tip of a lean forefinger almost touched the surface, moved a fraction of an inch above it to trace the small mouth. Thick black lashes almost hid the enigmatic blue-green of his eyes.

Once again Anet felt a swift wrench inside her, as though some fundamental force had altered her cellular structure, transforming her. She swallowed, held captive by the masculine strength of his finger against the soft pink and whiteness of the unknown woman's face.

He said, 'I think it was painted by her lover.'

Fortunately Scott strolled back into the room. 'All OK,' he said. 'Hello, what's this?'

'Olivia sent it to me,' Anet said woodenly.

Her nerves were tautly stretched. Yet nothing had happened. She had watched Lucas almost touch a painting, that was all. Her gaze fell on the portrait. Strange that she hadn't noticed the sympathy in the painted smile, or the tinge of smugness.

Lord, she thought, I'm losing my mind!

It was essential that she regain command of the situation. Saying quickly, 'I think I'd better ring Olivia and find out who this mysterious woman is!' she held out her hand.

Lucas didn't respond immediately; instead he looked at her with a hooded, elemental challenge that chilled her right through.

Then he smiled, irony and mockery nicely blended. Her outstretched hand shook slightly but she kept it extended. 'I'll take it with me,' she said lightly.

'If it's valuable,' Scott observed in a blessedly normal voice, 'we really should put it in a safety deposit box at the bank. There's no crime to speak of on Fala'isi, but just in case...'

Lucas put the portrait into her hand, his fingers brushing hers. Her skin seemed to have become thinner; she almost recoiled as sensation leapt from nerve-end to nerve-end through her body, setting it on fire.

'Thanks,' she said. 'I won't be long.'

Fala'isi and New Zealand were in the same time zone, so she got Olivia as she was preparing for dinner. 'I was just going to ring you!' she said, her voice golden with affection. 'Happy birthday!'

'Thank you. It's been a super one so far.' And then she stopped, because how could she tell Olivia that she didn't feel comfortable about accepting her gift?

But of course Olivia knew. With a little laugh she said, 'You think the portrait is too much.'

Thankfully, Anet took a deep breath and said, 'Olivia, it's absolutely beautiful and I love it, but I can't keep it. You must see that—even I can tell it's valuable.'

Olivia said warmly, 'I don't know whether it's genuine or not, but it's yours.'

'I can't accept it,' Anet protested. 'Olivia, does Drake—?'

'Agree? Of course he does. Truly, Anet, I haven't lost my mind. She's not a family heirloom. She's a—a good luck charm, I suppose you could call her.'

'Whatever, you must see that it's impossible for me to even think of—'

On an odd wry note, Olivia said, 'I don't know that you've got any choice, my dear. I think she knows where she wants to be.'

Anet's head came up. A shade brusquely she asked, 'What on earth do you mean?'

'Relax, relax. I'm not hinting at witchcraft or the occult. The lady is very determined, that's all. Anet, why not just keep her while you're in Fala'isi? If you really don't want her you can return her to me when you come back. All right?'

It wasn't all right, but Anet knew that she couldn't say so. Trying to banish the reluctance from her tone, she said, 'Yes, of course. And—thank you, Olivia.'

'Think of her as a temporary visitor,' Olivia said, laughter and a kind of understanding texturing her words. 'What do you think of Lucas Tremaine?'

'Overwhelming,' Anet returned drily.

'Isn't he just!'

Anet said, 'He's coming out to dinner with Scott and me tonight.'

'He's an interesting man,' Olivia said. 'I like him. So does Drake. He met him in San Rafael—Drake spent some time working in the mines there. He was delighted to see him again.'

'"Interesting" describes Lucas exactly,' Anet said, hoping she didn't sound as ambivalent as she felt. 'Olivia—'

'Have a wonderful night, Anet, and I hope this year is better than any other you've ever lived through. Yes, all right,' she said to someone else in the room, turning back to confide, 'I have to go now. Phillips has prepared a new dish and he's rather worried about it. I had to promise that Drake and I would be at the table dead on time!'

'Is Simon not at home?' Simon was Olivia's much younger half-brother, who lived with the Arundells.

'He's staying with a friend. Come and see us when you get back, Anet. All right, Phillips...'

The Arundells' manservant, housekeeper, nanny and good friend combined, a middle-aged man called simply Phillips, was a domestic tyrant who ruled the house with a rod of iron—especially when Olivia was pregnant, as she was now for the third time. Olivia and Drake hoped for a daughter to round off their family—'Although if it's another boy,' Olivia had said placidly the last time

Anet had seen her, 'I'll be perfectly happy. I like my boys.'

Anet was smiling as she hung up, but the smile faded as her eyes fell on the miniature. Tranquilly the small, exquisitely painted face gazed back at her.

'Young as you are, I think Olivia was right. You look to me,' Anet said, rewrapping her carefully, 'like someone to be reckoned with. I don't think you'd like the tropics—you're a Gainsborough lady, not a Gauguin. If Olivia's baby is a girl, I'll give you to her as a christening present.'

And she carried the parcel to her bedroom where, after some thought, she hid it in a drawer.

Compelled by an obscure impulse, she walked across her room to stand in front of the full-length mirror. 'Sturdy,' she told her reflection after several moment's scrutiny, 'describes you exactly. And solid.'

Everything about her was big—broad shoulders, wide hips, long, powerful legs. Since she'd given up field sports the heavy layers of muscle in her thighs and shoulders had sleeked down, but with her bone structure she'd never be anything but big.

'Just like your father,' her petite mother used to say, hugging her, unable to hide the note of regret in her voice.

Anet's eyes moved to examine her face with dispassionate interest. She was certainly no beauty, although she had her mother's pale, clear, fine skin. The best she could be called was striking, with her wide mouth and square jaw beneath cheekbones flaring away from a straight nose. Black short hair and barely arched brows contrasted shockingly with eyes of a light, limpid grey. If they'd been blue or brown their size would have been emphasised, but in spite of the curly dark lashes that surrounded them their transparency seemed to rob her of personality.

She and the woman in the miniature had nothing in common except their gender, she thought with a self-mocking smile. Not even in her cradle had she been called dainty. What on earth had made Olivia think she would like her gift?

Although perhaps Olivia knew her better than she did herself, because she did; she loved it.

Into her mind there popped Scott's words about Cara Tremaine. 'Beautiful...made you feel that just to be alive was a wonderful thing...'

Of course Lucas would marry an exceptional woman. Exceptional men did—it was the law of the jungle, or the survival of the fittest, or something. Alpha men married alpha women. She, as she had always known, was not an alpha woman. In fact, on occasion she had been the butt of remarks questioning her femininity; they had hurt when she was young, but she ignored them these days.

Which made the shivery inner feelings now assailing her ridiculous.

Perhaps some weakness in her made her fall passionately—futilely—in lust with tall, handsome men who possessed uncompromising authority and intense, bonedeep sexuality, men with charisma. And that, she thought derisively, was a much overrated word that meant nothing.

Anyway, Lucas was going to Hawaii, so she was safe.

Suddenly realising that she had been staring at her reflection with the still solemnity of a moonstruck owl— she, who never looked at herself except to comb her hair—she pulled a hideous face and walked out of the room.

Lucas and Scott were in the sitting room drinking beer. Both looked up as she came into the room, but it was Scott who demanded, 'What did she say?'

'If she weren't Olivia,' Anet answered thoughtfully, 'I'd say she was being cagey.'

Scott brought a glass of lime juice across to her. She'd have preferred wine, but when she'd found how much it cost on the island she'd blenched and given it up for the duration.

'That doesn't sound like Olivia,' Lucas commented, sounding amused and indulgent.

'No, it doesn't, but she wasn't exactly forthcoming.' She recounted Olivia's words.

'A whim,' Scott decided. 'She suddenly thought you'd like it.'

Anet suppressed her inchoate suspicion that there was more to the unexpected present than a mere feminine whim. Conjuring up a social smile copied from her mother, she turned to Lucas and said, 'Thank you very much for breaking your journey to deliver it.'

'It was nothing,' he said with negligent courtesy.

'You're too kind,' she said automatically, and felt heat run along her cheekbones and hairline at the subtly taunting smile he directed at her. Hurriedly she continued, 'Do you have your flight booked for Hawaii?'

'I had to cancel when I stopped off here, but it'll be easy enough to get another one.'

Scott put his glass down. 'How long do you think you'll be there?'

'Until I've finished my research. A week or so, I imagine, then I'll head back to New Zealand to write.' He drained his glass, throat muscles working. 'I have a house on a hill overlooking a beach on the Coromandel,' he said. 'It's primitive and isolated and gut-wrenchingly beautiful. Perfect for a writer.'

Scott nodded, then enquired after someone called Old Ropy, who'd been at school with them. Lucas didn't know where this improbably named person was, but Scott wasn't deterred. He mentioned other names, and they slipped into the sort of conversation that consisted mainly of, 'Do you remember...?' until Lucas said, 'We must be boring Anet rigid.'

Scott gave her a fond smile. 'Not Annie,' he said. 'She's very restful, is Annie. Doesn't drive a man crazy with her yattering all the time.'

'Don't talk about me as though I'm not here,' she said, laughing in spite of herself. 'And shouldn't we be going?'

CHAPTER THREE

SCOTT had not overpraised the restaurant. Although the big room was packed, and noisy with local Chinese families, islanders and tourists, and the clicking ceiling fans barely disturbed the humid, spice-scented air, the food was divine.

'Ambrosia,' Anet sighed as she lifted her bowl of jasmine tea in a silent toast to her cousin. 'One of the best meals I've ever tasted, anywhere.'

Scott looked pleased. 'I thought you'd like it. Serena and I come here whenever we feel rich.'

'I never stop being surprised at how extraordinarily well you can eat throughout the Pacific,' Lucas commented.

'You should write a book about it,' Scott said, grinning. '*Eating your way around the Pacific.* You'd have every armchair traveller in the world buying it.'

Lucas laughed. 'One day I might just do that.'

He'd been a good companion—witty, amusing and an excellent raconteur, and obviously enjoying the evening, yet Anet suspected that one part of him stood back and viewed the world with an unemotional, disinterested gaze, safe behind the barrier he'd constructed to keep the rest of humankind at a distance.

He didn't reveal much of himself in his books either. Although exciting and topical and searingly written, the personal outrage that must fuel his need to track down perpetrators of crime was always kept under vigilant control.

'Time to go,' Scott told them, getting to his feet as the waiter brought back the tray and his credit card. When the bill had arrived he and Lucas had exchanged a few cryptic remarks, from which Anet had gathered that Lucas would reimburse him later for his share.

Outside, breathing in air scented with the myriad odours of growth and fecundity, Anet realised that Lucas was to accompany them to the nightclub. Stop jittering, she told her stomach firmly as she looked out of the car windows at the thin line of white where the combers met the reef. As her legs were marginally shorter than his she had insisted on sitting in the back—which position, unfortunately for her peace of mind, gave her an excellent view of an autocratic, angular profile every time Lucas turned his head to speak.

The nightclub was quite skilfully decorated with a ceiling of thatched pandanus leaves so that it looked like a very large fale—one of the island's superbly simple traditional houses—and it hummed. Everyone under twenty-three on the island seemed to be there, dancing enthusiastically to a band that played a clever mixture of rock music and Hawaiian pop.

While they were being shown to a table she felt someone looking at her, and turned her head slightly to meet Georgia Sanderson's green eyes.

'Hi, there,' Scott said, professionally affable. 'Having fun?'

Looking back, Anet would never be sure exactly how Georgia did it, but within a minute, and so smoothly that no one had the chance to influence events, she and her friend Penny Reiver were sitting down at the same table and a waiter was taking their orders.

Scott, being Scott, thought it was a good idea. It was impossible to tell from Lucas's face what he thought, but his smile seemed perfectly genuine.

And why not? Anet thought as she watched them talk. Georgia was stunning, and Penny was tall and slender and amusing. Any normal man would be delighted to have them sit at his table.

Lethargy attacked Anet, alienating her from the infectious rhythm and the air of enormous good humour that permeated the room.

'And where did you eat?' Georgia asked Lucas after drinks had been ordered. Tonight she was too subtle to flutter her lashes, but they quivered.

A nice touch, Anet thought, shocked by her acerbic reactions.

'It's Anet's birthday so we went to The Jade Horse,' Scott told her cheerfully.

'Your birthday?' Georgia lifted her glass of orange juice. 'Many happy returns,' she said, smiling while her eyes appraised Anet's dress. 'How old are you today?'

'Twenty-five,' Anet said, angry with herself for being so unreasonably terse but unable to stop it.

'Oh.' Georgia surveyed her with her head tipped slightly to one side, a smile curling her ripe mouth, and said, 'I suppose it's your height that makes you look more mature. Sort of queenly.'

Anet decided to treat it as a compliment. 'That's the first time anyone has ever called me regal. Thank you.'

'This afternoon as I was in town looking at the shops I realised that this is the perfect place for you. The islanders are wonderful, aren't they? They move so slowly, like stately ships, and there are quite a few who are almost as tall as you are. You look really at home here.' When Georgia's eyes travelled on to rest limpidly on Lucas's face another note entered her voice. 'But you don't see many really tall men here.'

'The Polynesians are noted for their splendid build more than their height,' he said easily.

Deliberately Anet relaxed tense muscles. She had dealt with cattiness before, both at school and more recently on the sports field. It was no big deal. Nevertheless she was pleased when a young man stopped beside the table to ask Scott something about diving.

'Well, it'll take me a few minutes to tell you all about it. Why don't you join us?' Scott said expansively.

After one look at Georgia and Penny the newcomer said, 'I'll just go and get my mate. He's coming tomorrow as well.'

Georgia said nothing, but a flash of irritation crossing her face made her feelings obvious.

'That's what you do here,' Scott assured her, his earnest look a little too ingenuous to be authentic. 'It's a great place to make friends.'

'I am not,' Georgia returned swiftly, 'the sort of person who considers chance-met acquaintances to be friends.'

'Oh, so you knew Lucas before you arrived on Fala'isi?' Scott asked, all innocence.

Georgia said, 'No, but of course I know Jan.' She smiled sweetly at Anet. 'Very well indeed,' she drawled.

Game, set and match to Georgia, Anet thought drily. She met Lucas's eyes, the blue in them almost drowned out by green the intense colour of a kingfisher's head.

'Enjoying yourself?' he asked.

'Very much.'

'Do you like dancing?' He spoke idly, his eyes on a couple who were jitterbugging with an enviable lack of self-consciousness.

'Yes.'

Perhaps it was the baldness of her answer that caught his attention. His glance sharpened as it lingered on her face. 'I imagine you'd be good at it,' he said.

Awareness stroked Anet's nerves with a warm, knowing finger, sending shivery little sensations down her spine and into her bones—sensations that robbed her of strength and will. His eyes rested for a taut, silent moment on her mouth. To her shock she realised that every cell in her body was eagerly expectant.

Remember, he's a flirt, she told herself grittily. He can't help practising on every female he meets.

'I try not to tread on feet,' she said, the meaningless words echoing in her ears as she turned away from his disturbing eyes and far too handsome face to accept her drink from the waiter.

Unfortunately Scott, who was talking to the two young men, asked Lucas to verify a statement he'd made, and that left Anet to face Georgia's green gaze. 'You do get around,' the older woman observed, her tone only just not patronising.

Anet nodded. 'It goes with the job,' she returned amiably.

Georgia ran a perfectly manicured fingernail through her sleek red hair. 'Don't you find it dull, pandering to tourists all day?' she asked.

'It depends on the people,' Anet said truthfully.

'Well,' Georgia said with negligent assurance, 'I'd need a little more mental stimulation than that.'

She was, Anet recalled, some sort of publicity person. 'Don't you find Fala'isi exciting?'

'The scenery's stunning.' Georgia shrugged. 'For the rest—it's a bit like this, isn't it? Rather loud tourists enjoying themselves in an unsophisticated way. I thought there'd be some decent nightlife.'

Anet kept her face expressionless. 'There are a couple of upmarket nightclubs,' she observed.

'Filled with tourists.' She sent a disparaging look around the room. 'I believe some really interesting people spend their holidays here, but you'd never know. They certainly don't seem to go out at night.'

Anet discarded the idea of telling her that because celebrities tended to come to Fala'isi for privacy they usually stayed on secluded estates outside the little town. What on earth had possessed the woman to come here? Surely she'd be much happier celebrity-spotting in Monaco or Los Angeles?

Subduing exasperation, Anet said, 'Well, yes, I believe some do, although I'm afraid I don't know their haunts. I've only been here a short time myself. Why not try the beaches?'

'Always provided I can get onto a beach without being forced to cover myself in some greasy sludge,' Georgia flashed back.

'It is,' Anet said patiently, 'for your own good.'

Georgia's lashes flickered as she lowered them. 'I dislike doing things for my own good,' she purred. 'I'm afraid I enjoy a bit of danger—some spice of risk in my life.'

Lucas must have heard her. However, he ignored the provocative observation to say blandly, 'Anet, how about that dance you promised me?'

As if following a cue, the band swung into a slower set, giving the dancers a chance to cool down and get to know each other better. Without making an issue about never having promised Lucas a dance, Anet rose and went with him onto the floor. Just before the lights dimmed she noticed that their departure seemed to have acted as some sort of signal. Both Georgia and her friend were following them with the two young men, leaving Scott to get to his feet and head towards a group of slightly older people.

The insistent rhythm of the drums permeated the music, and there was a lazily sensuous intimacy in the singer's voice that beguiled and beckoned into reck-lessness, heating Anet's blood and scrambling her thoughts. Looking around the room, she realised that she and Lucas were the two tallest people there. After a lifetime of dancing with men who were shorter than herself, or the same height, it felt odd to be with a man whose face she had to look up to see.

The muscles of Lucas's shoulder flexed beneath Anet's hand. She kept her face as wooden and expressionless as she could, because being held close to him stirred a heated, primitive expectation into life.

'I was right,' Lucas murmured, holding her firmly but not too close. 'You dance like an Amazon.'

Her head came up; instead of looking decidedly over his shoulder her eyes searched his. 'Amazons were not particularly feminine,' she said. 'They were belligerent, and noted for their ferocity and skill in battle. I'm sure they'd have thought dancing a frivolous, useless pastime.'

'Nonsense. They must have been overwhelmingly seductive because they had to lure men from neighbouring tribes to make love to them and father their children. Either the women of the neighbouring tribes were incredibly complaisant—especially as any sons were sent back to them to rear—or the Amazons were so irresistible that the men thought the subsequent uproar from their own women worth it.'

Was he teasing her? Of course he was; his hard mouth had relaxed into a half-smile, and amusement glinted in the kingfisher-coloured eyes.

'I thought they kidnapped young girls to replenish the tribe,' she said, wishing she'd spent more time reading Greek mythology.

'They bore children and only kept the daughters. Whom I'm sure they taught to dance. Seductively.'

He was a flirt.

If she kept that in mind she'd be all right. He probably discussed slightly *risqué* myths with every woman he danced with.

And it was stupid to feel this strong, elemental tug at her senses. She had nothing to offer a man who so effortlessly caught every feminine eye in the room.

'It's an interesting theory,' she said dismissively, trying hard to regulate her heartbeat. It was quite unfair that he was able to smash through her common sense and determination and self-control to ignite such an indiscreet, irresistible hunger. For some reason—possibly his size, she thought acidly—her body had recognised in Lucas Tremaine a man she wanted.

She didn't make the mistake of underestimating her response, but while straightforward physical lust might be embarrassing it wasn't dangerous—unless she mistook it for love.

And she wasn't going to do that.

He laughed softly, sending odd little streamers of fire through her. 'Actually, when I first saw you at the Olympics I thought that that was how the goddesses must

have seemed to ancient people—larger than life, forbidding, and awe-inspiring in their physical perfection.'

Astounded, she kept her eyes fixed on the brightly
coloured clothes of the dancers across the room. Scott
had been right; the sarongs were out in vivid profusion.
'No one is physically perfect,' she pointed out, making
her voice as prosaic as she could, wondering why he was
lying to her. Did he want something from her? And if
so, what?

'You come close to it.'

The music changed to sexy, vibrant pop, slow enough
to be arousing, fast enough to loosen inhibitions and too
noisy to converse over. Thank God, Anet thought. She
could plead tiredness, say she wanted to sit down, but
that would be giving in, and she wasn't trained to surrender. This game of cat and mouse, if that was what
it was, set her teeth on edge. She looked around, trying
to fix her mind on something.

And saw, just in front of them, Georgia dance away
from her partner, a study in sensuousness, her slender
body flowing, undulating in a message that was both
seductive and taunting. Her eyes flicked up to Lucas,
and on her mouth was a sly, significant smile.

Admiration glinted in his glance. Even as Anet stiffened he pulled her closer, and for a moment she yielded.

Only for a moment, because she felt the hard shock
of his arousal and knew that it was Georgia who had
caused it.

Revulsion, keen and bitter, stabbed her. Abruptly, exerting her not inconsiderable strength, she pulled back.
Lucas looked down at her, his brilliant eyes once more
unreadable.

'I'd like to sit down,' she mouthed.

He nodded, took her elbow and set off through the
crowd of pulsating dancers. As had happened on the
boat, people got out of his way automatically.

It must be great to have such authority, Anet thought
furiously, sickened by her naïvety, angry with him. Yet

why should she blame him because he found Georgia
attractive? It was her own fault if she'd spun a few
fancies, let herself dream a short dream.

A waiter hurried to pull out her chair. She sat down
and picked up her glass, drinking the orange juice deeply
before setting it down again. Georgia and her partner
had moved and were dancing close by. Anet felt an ignoble satisfaction as she noted the dark streaks in the
red hair, the glisten of moisture beneath Georgia's chiselled nose and across her temples.

'So tell me,' Lucas said blandly, 'how you get to be
an Olympic class athlete in field events.'

Anet dragged her eyes away from the other woman
and looked down at her broad, competent hand on the
table. In an impersonal voice she said, 'You need the
build to begin with, of course—the height and the big
bones—but it's amazing what exercise and the right food
can do. When I was competing I went up two sizes—'
Mortified, she stopped, colour heating her cheekbones.
Her head felt heavy on the taut muscles of her neck.

'Go on,' he said.

For some obscure reason that laconic command increased her tension. Forcing her mouth into a smile, she
said, 'And you need a good coach—but sheer, bloody-
minded, bull-headedness is probably the greatest asset
an athlete can have.'

'You must have sacrificed a lot of things ordinary
people take for granted.' He waited for a second before
adding, 'Of course, the rewards are great. Which is one
of the reasons, I suppose, why so many athletes resort
to drugs to get to the top.' He was watching her with
lazy interest.

'Where there's money and fame,' she said shortly,
'there will always be people who want to take the easy
way to get them.'

His expression didn't alter, although his voice was
considering, almost pensive. 'I find this adulation of
athletes very interesting. Apart from the fact that the

rise in feminism seems to have coincided with the acceptance of women in sport and athletics, there's the interesting fact that every civilisation which has paid its athletes has fallen.'

She thought that over, then pointed out, 'Every civilisation prior to this one, whether its athletes have been paid or not, has fallen. That's what happens to civilisations. They rise and then they fall. As for feminism...' She smiled ironically. 'Another interesting fact about the status of women is that within a hundred years of the arrival of romantic novels women were choosing their own husbands instead of having them chosen for them by other people.'

'Do you think the two are connected?'

She shrugged. 'Connected, certainly. I doubt if one caused the other. The times were moving that way.'

'Brains as well,' he said, a note in his voice catching her attention.

She sent him a startled glare. Had he been testing her? 'What did you expect?' she retorted crisply. 'The myth of the dumb ox with all his brains in his muscles is long past its due date.'

'So as well as determination and single-mindedness an athlete needs intelligence. A formidable set of attributes. It must make them uncomfortable to be around.'

She smiled sardonically. 'They aren't necessarily noted for the sweetness of their temper.'

'And where does a sense of fair play fit into all this?'

Anet didn't like the way he spoke. Of course he'd be aware of the rumours; it was more than possible that he believed them. However, when she looked up his face was bland and the turquoise eyes revealed nothing, their opacity both alarming and infuriating.

'Athletes are like the rest of humanity,' she said evenly, fighting down a ridiculous disappointment. 'Some have a high moral code, a few don't.'

'And to those few a sense of fair play is rather like giving aid and succour to the enemy,' he suggested. 'So they use intimidation.'

'You have to train yourself to deal with anything that comes along. But often,' she added sweetly, recalling that he had been a journalist, 'that sort of thing is found only in the minds of journalists desperate to drum up readers.'

Waiting for the inevitable question, she braced herself, but he said merely, 'I'd like to talk your athletic career over with you some time, if you don't mind.'

Quick, heart-felt relief was immediately followed by cynical speculation. He could be lulling her into accepting him as harmless. Hot on the heels of that suspicion came the thought that it sounded as though he intended to stick around for a while.

Stung by the spurt of—pleasure? No, that was too colourless a word to describe the emotion, sweet and drugging as wine, that swirled through her veins—she shrugged and said nonchalantly, 'Why not?'

He smiled, the hard, beautiful mouth twisting slightly. 'I'll hold you to that,' he said gently, somehow making the words sound like a threat.

Anet hoped she wasn't setting herself up for a fall.

Fortunately Georgia and her partner arrived back then, and within a few minutes Lucas asked the redhead to dance and they left the table.

Determinedly pinning a smile to her mouth, Anet turned to the young man beside her and asked, 'How are you enjoying Fala'isi?'

Conversation didn't prove to be difficult. Dazzled at the thought of talking to a woman who had shaken hands with presidents and royalty, he asked her eager questions. This she could deal with. Recounting a few carefully chosen anecdotes, making him laugh, helped keep her eyes resolutely away from the dance-floor, where Georgia chatted vivaciously with Lucas as they danced. The obligatory sarong suited her to perfection, the vivid golds and greens of the material setting off her crown of hair and the drape of the skirt revealing elegant legs.

The young man ordered mineral water for Anet and another beer, and as she sipped the cool, mildly salty liquid he told her about himself and what he planned to do and the fun he was having on this holiday. He was pleasant and cheerful and Anet enjoyed talking to him—especially when she moved her chair so that she had her back to the dancers.

Eventually, when the music had slowed to a smooth, smoochy number, he leaned forward and said, 'Getting gold must have been the high point of your life.'

Anet almost laughed at the sudden embarrassment that flooded his face. Clearly, he'd remembered too late what had followed the Olympic Games.

Lifting her glass to her lips to hide her bitter smile, Anet sipped before producing her stock reply. 'I devoutly hope not! It would be an appalling thing to reach the pinnacle of your life when you're only twenty. Think of all those years stretching ahead, with only downhill to go.'

'I hadn't thought of that,' he said. 'But you're right. I'll look at the little gymnasts on the dais with a different eye now.'

From behind Anet came Lucas's unexpected voice. 'Most of them manage quite well. Anet, for example, is a physiotherapist.'

His words startled Anet; somehow they gave the impression that she and Lucas knew each other much better than they really did.

'Oh,' Georgia said, sinking into a chair, 'I forgot, Annie. While you and Lucas were dancing a person came around selling things.' Directing a sharp, bright smile at Anet, she groped in her bag. 'Here,' she said, removing a small parcel wrapped in bright blue tissue paper and holding it out. 'Happy birthday!'

Because she couldn't do anything else, Anet took it. 'Thank you,' she said, trying to sound surprised and delighted. It wasn't enough so she added lamely, 'What a lovely thought.'

Georgia laughed. 'Open it, do.'

Inside was a choker-length string of glass beads made to look like the island's famed black pearls. Copying her mother, who knew how to deal with everything, Anet said, 'Oh, they are pretty. Thank you, Georgia, that's really sweet of you!'

'Put them on,' Georgia insisted, smiling.

The string was too short to suit her; it would make her neck look short and muscular. Anet slid the string over her hand, gave it a couple of turns around her wrist and held out her arm. 'There,' she said. 'The local pearls are unique, aren't they?'

'Very,' Georgia said dulcetly.

Uncomfortably, Anet picked up her glass, glad that the music had finished so that Penny and her partner rejoined them, both flushed and clearly pleased with themselves and each other.

Scott, too, appeared. 'Annie, can I drag you away for a moment?' When Lucas looked up he said, 'We'll only be a short time.'

Lucas nodded and turned back to Georgia. Relieved, Anet went with her cousin.

His friends, a small group of locals, greeted her with enthusiasm. No one mentioned the Olympics, or her medal, or rumours. In their undemanding company the screw of tension inside her slowly began to ease.

Steadfastly she refused to look at the group around the other table. More than once she heard Georgia's breathless laugh. Although she felt big and obvious, standing there in her shirtwaister when everyone else was attired in their varying ideas of South Seas chic, she held her shoulders erect and smiled and talked and enjoyed herself.

Some time later Scott looked at his watch. 'Lord,' he said, shocked, 'we'd better be going home, Annie—we've got to get up at the crack of dawn.'

Goodbyes said, he bustled Anet away, waving to other friends and tourists he'd taken out, his wide, honest smile expressing nothing but pleasure. There were no secrets with Scott; what you saw was what you got. Anet loved him for his openness and transparent good humour, so different from Lucas's compelling composure, with its dangerous undercurrent of fire beneath the control.

'I wonder if Lucas wants to stay,' he said. 'He seems quite smitten with the lady.'

Lucas was sitting with his golden-brown head bent towards Georgia as they talked. They were alone at the table. As they came up Anet saw his mouth curl in a breathtaking smile and winced at the sudden contraction somewhere in the region of her heart.

He saw them before Georgia did, getting to his feet with a negligent grace that reminded her of a large predator, all contained strength and leashed motion.

'We're off,' Scott said. 'Catch you later, Georgia.'

Either she hadn't come across the colloquialism before or she disapproved of it. One fine eyebrow lifted. Graciously, not smiling, she said, 'Goodbye, and thank you for a very pleasant trip out to the reef.'

Scott turned to Lucas, but before he could say anything his friend said coolly, 'I'll walk back to my hotel.'

Anet didn't miss Georgia's veiled air of triumph. A deep, still anger at her own stupidity gave her the fortitude to say, 'Goodnight, Georgia. Enjoy the rest of your holiday. Goodnight, Lucas.'

'See you around, mate,' Scott said to Lucas, shaking hands with him.

Lucas smiled. 'Goodnight.'

Outside, Scott took the car keys from his pocket. 'Great place, eh?' he said as he inserted them in the lock. 'Don't think the pretty Georgia liked it much, though. It doesn't seem her style.'

The heavy sweetness of frangipani swirled hypnotically around Anet. 'I think she hoped for a little more sophistication—somewhere exclusive,' she said gravely, adding with a note of malice, 'A place the uncouth and exuberant hoi polloi can't get into.'

'Well, she's not likely to find anyone more sophisticated than Lucas,' Scott said stoutly.

'I think she's quite happy with Lucas,' Anet returned.

Once in the car she sat with her lips firmly closed, but before they had left the main street of the little city she asked casually, 'Whereabouts in New Zealand does Lucas come from? I don't think I know his family.'

'He's a Mainlander,' Scott told her, using the New Zealanders' affectionate nickname for the South Island. 'His father was a very important diplomat, Sir William Tremaine. Lucas grew up in embassies all around the world, but his parents sent him to secondary school in Christchurch. He was going to be a diplomat too—he took his degree at Oxford—but for some reason he decided he'd rather be a journalist instead.

'Shocked the hell out of his parents—they didn't speak to him for years—but Lucas has never been the sort of person to be intimidated into anything. Even at school he went his own way. Anyway, he was a damned good journalist. Then he went to San Rafael, just because he was curious about a nasty little tinpot war they were having. Cara's family was mixed up in it somehow. Anyway, Lucas smuggled her out and married her.'

'And it was her death that led to his first book,' she said with a shiver. 'Poor Lucas.'

'Cara's death changed something in him. He was always tough, but that really hardened him. You've read his books, I suppose?'

'Yes. They're excellent, very well written. Grim, though. I wouldn't exactly say that I enjoyed them.'

'Well, he's got good reason not to think much of humanity.'

'No wonder he enjoys solitude,' she said, thinking of his long, solo voyages around the Pacific.

He said a little enviously, 'He's always been a wanderer. I think he was born in the wrong age. I can imagine him discovering new continents—'

'Looting and plundering,' she said acidly, knowing she was being unfair. 'A pirate.'

He said swiftly, 'No, you've read him wrong. He's a good man, Lucas—I'd trust him with my life—but something died in him when Cara was killed. He just doesn't seem to give a damn any more. Not that it stops women from chasing him unmercifully—they always did, even at school. I suppose it's that damn-your-eyes look.'

It was more than that, but she wasn't going to try and explain it to Scott! Cara Tremaine must have been quite a woman, because it would have taken someone special to tame that buccaneering heart.

The engine note changed as Scott swung the car into the narrow driveway beside the house. Walking into the small sitting room, with its cane sofa and armchairs, Anet said, 'One thing I've never been able to get used to in the tropics is all those indoor plants growing in the backyard.'

He grinned. 'They look just like other plants to me— green and leafy. Serena likes them, though. Goodnight, Annie. See you in the morning.'

In the second bedroom she took off her clothes with short, sharp movements, resisting the temptation to dump them on the other bed. Her mother and Jan were particularly tidy, and over the years she'd been coaxed and prodded into copying them. When she'd hung her clothes up she wrapped her cotton dressing gown around her and headed for the bathroom. Tomorrow she'd find the time to go to the local gym, she decided. It was too hot to run here, and although she swam for half an hour each evening it wasn't enough to keep her as fit as she was accustomed to being.

She climbed into the bed, grateful that her feet didn't hang over the end—how did Lucas manage? she wondered sleepily. There couldn't be many beds that accommodated his length comfortably. Perhaps he had to sleep from corner to corner...

Afterwards she blamed that last, vagrant thought for the dream. That, and the miniature he had delivered, so evocative of eighteenth-century beauty.

It started innocently enough: she was riding through an English night in a horse-drawn coach, peering worriedly at the darkened countryside. It was imperative that she reach her destination—although she didn't know where she was going—so she had to risk travelling along this highwayman-infested stretch of road. Tensely, her hands folded in her silk-clad lap, she strained to hear above the clatter of the wheels on the rough road.

Somehow she knew what was going to happen but, as was always the way in dreams, in spite of all her efforts she couldn't command her body so that she could order the coach back.

Inevitably the call to 'Stand and deliver!' rang out.

Terrified, Anet knew that her only hope was to open the door on the far side and slip out, but apart from the rapid, heavy thud of her heart in her throat she was locked in stasis.

Eyes dilating, she watched as the door on her side of the coach was wrenched open, and a hand dragged her down the two steps and out onto the stony road. A sick fear churned her stomach as she was forced to stand there in the pale moonlight and look at the man whose strong fingers were clamped about her wrist.

'So, lady?' the highwayman said, his double-caped cloak swirling around his tall form. Dark hair was gathered neatly behind his head, and beneath the cloak gleamed a white shirt with ruffles at the neck and at the cuffs of the full sleeves. 'What do you have to deliver to me?'

She tried to speak, but her mouth dried so that the words couldn't be produced. Racked by fear, she gazed into eyes that burned behind a black mask. And as she was captured by the intensity of those eyes she realised that this man had known she was coming, that the encounter was not just bad luck. He had been waiting for her. She was his prey.

'Well, my pretty,' he growled, his voice oddly familiar and yet not, 'do you refuse to speak to a common highwayman?'

At this her courage surged back. 'What could I have to say to someone like you?' she demanded.

'You could plead sweetly to be freed.'

'And would you do it?' She heard the soft movements of a horse's restless hooves, the muted clink of harness, yet she saw nothing but the glitter of purpose in the man's eyes.

'Nay, lady,' he said, and laughed deep in his throat, his fingers tightening on her wrist as he brought her up against him.

He smelt pleasantly of horse and fresh sweat. Stunned by an unknown complex of sensations, she froze as his arms caged her. He was smiling, his teeth white and regular. Suddenly aware of danger, she began to struggle. Yet although she was afraid she wasn't repelled.

She lifted a wrathful face and saw that maddening smile. He was playing with her.

'I have nothing for you,' she said coldly.

'I give you the lie, lady.' His arms contracted around her and she was forced to confront the perfidy of her own responses. Heat enveloped her; she wanted nothing more than to surrender.

'But not here, not now,' he said, and bent his head and kissed her, his mouth hard and possessive as though he knew her well, as though she were his for the taking, as though something more than mere lust joined them.

His mouth on hers was searingly intrusive, but not so much as the fierce parting of her lips and the shocking mating of tongues. Fire leapt through her.

At last he set her away from him.

'You are mine,' he said harshly, his voice a little troubled by the rapid lift and fall of his chest. 'Do not

forget that, lady. For if you do I will have to remind
you, and you will not like the way I do it. I will come
for you when I am ready.'

'You cannot—'

He interrupted her biting response with laughter, yet
there was no amusement in his voice when he said, low
and intense and deep, 'Lady, you do not know what I
can do. Make sure that you do not force me to show
you.'

Dumbly, she watched him swing up onto the coal-black
horse and sketch a salute in the moonlight before setting
spurs to the animal's sleek hide. Long after it disappeared she heard the thunder of its hoofbeats echoing
down the days of her life...

Still unable to move, every muscle held in thrall, Anet
at last managed to force open her eyes. She stared at the
window, pale now with approaching dawn. In the transient dimness she could see the familiar outlines of the
furniture in Scott and Serena's house on Fala'isi.

Dragging herself out of bed, she padded across the
room and pulled back the curtains, and with her heart
thundering in her chest she watched the sun leap above
the horizon, thrusting long fingers of light through the
smooth, curved palm trunks.

Of all the futile, Freudian dreams, she thought, totally
disgusted with herself. One dance with a handsome man,
and you spend the rest of the night dreaming about him.

But, oh, it had seemed so real.

The shrill summons of the telephone had her racing
across her room to open the door, but Scott got there
first. Often the travel people at various hotels rang at
ungodly hours to organise trips for their guests. Without
closing the door properly, she went over to her dressing
table.

A couple of moments later an altered note in Scott's
voice caught her attention. Dropping her hairbrush onto
the bed, she hurried out into the sitting room. He was

a little pale, and his eyes were unfocused beneath drawn brows.

'Look, don't worry, darling,' he was saying urgently, 'I'll get there as soon as I can. No, it's all right! You're far more important to me than the business—anyway, I think I can see a way to deal with that.'

When Anet turned back to her room he looked up and motioned her to stay. 'I'll see you as soon as I can get there,' he said. 'Keep your chin up, sweet. She's a tough old bird; she'll be all right.'

'Her mother?' Anet asked anxiously as he put the receiver down.

He passed his hand over his unshaven jaw. 'Yeah. Serena was ringing from the hospital. They're worried. I have to go to Melbourne, Annie.'

'Of course you do,' she said practically. 'What can I do?'

'Exactly what you have been doing. I'll ring Lucas and see if he'll take my place.'

'But what about—? Oh, no, none of the men can take over from you, can they?'

'No, but Lucas has his boatmaster's. If he'll do it that will save me worrying about cancelling.' He looked up the hotel number and began to punch in the digits.

'Lucas?' he said. 'Listen, Lucas, I need a favour...'

The aftermath of the dream lingered like a drug, suffocating Anet's usual good sense. Stiffly, she went back to her room, closing the door behind her. The last thing she wanted was for Lucas Tremaine to take over from Scott. He was far too great a risk. Their odd, tense conversation the preceding evening about athletes still reverberated in her mind, overlaid by her contempt at his overt use of the charm he wielded like a weapon, and an unwanted, acute excitement.

Early though it was in the morning, the languorous, sultry heat of the South Seas seeped into her bones, slowing her movements, casting a patina of glamour over the day. Anet drew a deep breath and picked up her hairbrush again.

It would be too easy to let that lazy enchantment blind her to reality. And a very real question had just occurred to her.

Had Lucas been trying to persuade her to trust him, so that one day he could ask her why she had arranged the kidnapping of her greatest rival just before the Olympic Games?

CHAPTER FOUR

'LUCAS says he'll do it,' Scott called from the hallway a few moments later.

She opened the door. 'Good,' she said, surprised at how genuine her cheerfulness sounded.

'He's going to stay here,' he said, frowning at his wallet.

'Why?' The syllable cracked through the quietness.

He looked taken aback. 'He just said he would. I'm sorry, Annie, I didn't think you'd mind—don't you like him?'

Sometimes the nicest of men could be alarmingly thick.

'It's not that,' she said, choosing words with care, 'but living in the same house as someone is not the same as meeting them socially, you know.'

'Oh, if that's all...' Scott relaxed. 'Honestly, Annie, you're far too old for such a prissy outlook. Lucas is housetrained. In fact, as he's spent so much time on a boat, he's probably tidier than you are.'

Shocked by the intensity of her feelings, she realised that although it was partly caused by irritation at Scott's blindness, more was triggered by pain. Clearly it didn't occur to Scott that there was the remotest chance of Lucas finding her attractive enough to seduce.

But then, why should he? Influenced by that damned dream she'd overreacted. Oh, Lucas had used his merciless charm on her as he did on every other woman, but it would dissipate like frost in the sunlight when he was faced with the banality of sharing a bathroom and kitchen with her.

And the last thing she should do was worry poor old Scott; he had enough to concern him.

'I'm sure he is,' she said, forcing her voice into its normal calmness. 'Now, do you want me to organise a flight to Australia while you pack?'

Scott brightened. 'If you wouldn't mind, love.'

Without too much trouble she got him a seat on a plane leaving in an hour for Fiji, where he could pick up a jumbo jet which would get him to Sydney three-quarters of an hour before a plane left for Melbourne. After a moment's thought she telephoned the number Serena had left; it must have been a phone in the waiting room at the hospital because it was Serena who answered.

'Thanks,' she said simply, when Anet told her of the arrangements. 'I know I shouldn't drag him away, but I need him, Annie. More than we need the money.'

'Of course you do. Anyway, there's no need to worry,' Anet said reassuringly. 'Lucas Tremaine is going to take the boat out. Between us we'll be fine.'

Serena's voice wobbled. 'That will take a load off both our minds. Where would we be without our friends? Annie, I know we've thanked you before—'

'Don't be an idiot. You concentrate on getting your mother through this and don't worry about things here.'

Serena drew an audible breath. 'Oh, Annie, she looks so sick...'

'Just hang on in there. Scott will be with you soon.'

It didn't seem much comfort to give, but Serena's voice steadied. 'I know. I'm all right, really. Thank Lucas for me, won't you? Neither of you will ever know how much your help means.'

Her words echoed in Anet's brain as she put down the receiver. Any new business, especially one where the competition was as fierce as it was in the tourism world, needed careful nurturing. It was sheer good luck that Lucas had turned up at exactly the right time to help Scott, and she couldn't let her feelings queer the pitch.

After a glance at her watch she muttered a curse. She needed to get going. In less than an hour one of the boys would be taking the van from the depot to pick up clients from the various hotels and motels.

Each evening she and Scott and two of the islanders rinsed all the gear in fresh water, refilled the dive bottles, and scrutinised every regulator, buoyancy compensator, mask and fin for anything that could possibly lead to gear failure. And each morning began with another swift inspection to make sure that everything that could possibly be needed was there. As well, she rechecked every dive bottle with a pressure gauge.

'The customers,' Serena had said, 'get shirty if they go down and find they've only got ten minutes of air left!'

A beep from outside brought her head around. 'The taxi's here,' she called.

Scott appeared, looking harried. 'I've written down a list of things to do,' he said, handing it over, 'and I'll probably think of more while I'm flying, so I'll ring you tonight. Lucas will have the final responsibility, because he's the only one with the right qualifications, but the islanders know boats and the sea so you can trust them completely.' He gave her a hard hug, picked up his case and disappeared through the door.

Anet dressed, then grabbed her bag and her hat and went out into the kitchen, where she stuffed bread into the toaster and set the coffee brewing.

Twenty minutes later as she locked the door behind her, a taxi stopped outside on the street. An odd sensation uncurled in the pit of her stomach as Lucas paid the driver and strode towards her along the short drive, looking big and lean and dangerously purposeful.

After a swift intake of breath she manufactured a composed smile and said, 'Good morning.'

Those enigmatic eyes slid over her in a comprehensive survey that sent a tremor through her. Stop it, she told herself sternly. Dreams have no business in real life, and that was all it was—a dream called from some murky recess of her unconscious.

'Good morning. Ready to go, I see.'

'Yes, I have to check the equipment.' As the taxi slid away she asked, 'Where's your luggage?'

'It's arriving from the hotel this evening,' he said casually. 'Do we collect the customers?'

'No, Tera does that.' She glanced at the sturdy waterproof watch on her wrist. 'We're supposed to meet him with the list at the wharf in ten minutes.'

He held out his hand for the car keys, and when she didn't immediately give them to him said evenly, 'I thought you were in a hurry.'

Typical macho man, she thought, handing them over. She made sure she'd locked the door properly while he backed the car from its position beneath the lush, windtorn leaves of the thicket of banana palms. Although he'd probably never driven anything as old and cantankerous as Scott's vehicle before, he dealt with it efficiently, not swearing or stamping on the accelerator when it decided to cough asthmatically and grumble to a stop.

Impatience wasn't his style, she thought as he restarted it. His books revealed his patience, that of a hunter stalking prey—controlled, yet remorseless as death. He leaned over and opened the car door and she got in, trying to ignore the slow shiver of foreboding down her spine.

People were stirring everywhere in the little town. Down by the waterfront growers were selling to housewives and housegirls and those few self-catering tourists who were prepared to rise so early and shelve enough of their inhibitions to haggle joyously.

It was a noisy, gaudy scene; as well as the bright, alien hues of the produce, every islander was dressed in cottons that outshone a tropical sunset, and most had a hibiscus tucked behind one ear, the silken flowers vibrating with colourful intensity against generally dark hair.

Amidst laughter people shouted comments and insults to each other, and proffered vegetables and fruit—pink-flushed mangoes, golden and green hands of bananas and plantains, round green cannonballs of breadfruit, smooth-skinned pawpaws—twice the size of the small mountain pawpaws that grew in New Zealand, and so much sweeter—and great rough roots of taro.

In one area fish were spread out, gleaming bounty from the sea, their distinctive smell fighting it out with the scent of coconut oil from the processing plant. Later in the morning the trade winds would blow the aroma away, but at the moment it was like a rich, stifling blanket.

'I always feel as though I'm encased in coconut ice,' Lucas commented.

Anet laughed. 'Exactly. Like the sulphur smell in Rotorua.'

'Not in the least like that,' he said. 'This is pleasant; Rotorua smells like rotten eggs.'

'If you want to see geysers and mud pools you have to put up with the smell. Anyway, it only takes a day to get so used to it that you don't smell it any more—although I believe it's sheer hell if you're a perfume nose or a wine-taster. I met a chef once who said he simply couldn't cook in Rotorua because he couldn't smell what he was doing.'

'Was that the chef at the awards?' he asked casually. 'I saw you on television.'

Anet flushed. Two months ago she had been honoured, along with several other New Zealanders, for her contributions to the country's image overseas. Normally she'd have considered the whole thing a tourist and publicity exercise, but this particular award meant a lot to her, for it indicated that she was at last living down the rumours.

'Yes, it was.'

'You seemed to be getting on like a house on fire.'

'He was a nice chap,' she said, 'but he just hated the food at the banquet, and kept threatening to erupt in a heated diatribe. I had to talk fast to keep his mind off it. In the end he found something in the sauce that he couldn't identify, so he spent ages happily trying to work out what it was.'

Lucas's hard mouth quirked. 'Leaving you free to enjoy the occasion. You looked as though you were having a magnificent time. Poised and confident and very happy.'

'I was happy,' she agreed, 'once I'd thanked everyone. Until then I was just very, very nervous. I didn't want to offend anyone by leaving them out, but I couldn't bear the thought of standing there for ten minutes while I read out a list of people who had helped me.'

'You did it very well,' he said. 'Short enough to retain interest, long enough not to sound perfunctory, a little touch of humour and a bit of sentimentality. It was a well-judged speech.'

Although she could discern nothing in his expression, or in those disturbingly inscrutable eyes, some under-note in his tone scraped along her nerves. The only safe way to deal with his comment was to treat it at face value.

'Thank you,' she said remotely. 'If that's so, I more than fulfilled what I set out to do; all I hoped for was sincerity and not to bore too many people.'

'Instead, you charmed them utterly,' he said, avoiding a large woman on a very small motor scooter who was puttering down the middle of the road with all the dash of a Formula One contender, a toddler held firmly in the small of her back by a large swathe of hibiscus-patterned cotton.

He had quick reflexes. And he was good behind the wheel—anticipating the vagaries of the traffic as well as those of the pedestrians, who all seemed to put their faith in the ability of some supernatural power to protect them from their complete lack of respect for road rules.

'And looked stunning while you did it,' he added smoothly.

'Thank you,' she said again, feeling stupid. She knew she'd looked good in the black and silver dress, but she also knew that the television camera was cruel to those who weren't reed-thin, and she had no illusions.

Perhaps 'stunning' was another way of saying 'much better than anyone your size could be expected to look'.

And you can stop that right now, she told herself sternly. It had been years since she'd dithered about the effect she had on anyone, and it worried her that she should be doing it now. It gave Lucas too much importance.

Unfortunately it was proving difficult to prise him from her brain. That damned dream, for example, was nothing—merely a fantasy triggered by the miniature— yet she'd responded to it like a superstitious adolescent! It was just plain ridiculous, and it would have to stop.

Of course, she decided, cheering up slightly, the boring, day-to-day grind of working together and living in the same house would soon free her from this humiliating response to Lucas's male mystique. It took a really determined man to look sexy and dangerous when shaving. The few crushes she'd had while she was competing had fizzled out under the pressure of living in training camps and seeing the objects of her desire at close quarters, all mystery and glamour driven away by the relentless exigencies of the everyday.

'That,' he said, pulling into the kerb outside the wharf area, 'is a singularly interesting expression on your face.'

The sun was still low, outlining the hard, flat angles and planes of his face. To Anet's dazzled eyes he looked for a moment like some ancient god, earthbound yet still cloaked in privilege and power and ruthlessness.

'I was working out what I have to do,' she said, driven to lie by a sense of self-preservation, her confidence seeping away under the ironic, unsettling regard of his blue-green eyes.

'Really?' he said, and switched off the engine.

Between them, helped by the members of the family who had been rostered on for that day, they readied the

boat and the equipment just in time to greet the divers
as they arrived.

When they were all aboard Lucas took the boat out
through the reef so skilfully that no spray reached a single
bikini or any of the slick, heated skin bared so conspicu-
ously by almost everyone on board.

He was a hit, Anet thought sardonically. His uncompromising male charisma more than made up for his lack
of Scott's friendly openness.

'I'll stay on board,' Lucas told her when the boat was
anchored, surveying the horizon with a mariner's eye.
'It could come up to rain later, and where there's rain
there's usually wind.'

It made sense. 'I've already divided them into two
groups,' she said, looking the divers over. 'The German
group and the Australians are experts; they'll be all right
by themselves. I'll take the rest on a resort dive.'

'What about the New Zealanders?'

She gave him a startled, respectful glance. So he'd
noticed too. From their conversation she'd gathered that
the man and the woman were not a couple, simply travelling with a party, the rest of whom had decided to stay
ashore that day. However, something about their body
language had struck her as doubtful.

'They showed me their certificates,' Anet said slowly,
watching as the woman pushed windswept hair into
place; it was long and straight, gleaming blue-black in
the sunlight.

'But?'

'Oh, I'm probably being silly. I just thought the man's
attitude was a bit suspect, but all he's been doing is
boasting about his prowess as a spear-fisherman, and
plenty do that. I'll see if they'll come with me on the
resort dive, but if they don't want to they can go with
the Germans and the Australians.'

'I'm going to enjoy seeing you as a mother duck,' he
said, smiling.

Her heart lifted. That rare, uncomplicated smile was something else again. Averting her face in case she revealed how much it affected her, she cast a knowledgeable eye over the clients. 'It's not diving, really,' she said. 'It's always fun, though. The corals here are absolutely exquisite, and everyone loves the fish. They're so used to divers they're almost completely tame.'

The customers were ready, so she pulled her T-shirt over her head. Beneath it she wore a sleek one-piece bathing suit in royal blue. Lucas had been surveying the two New Zealanders, but when she picked up the sunscreen he turned his head.

Anet's skin tightened, and a slow, helpless tide of colour heated her breasts and flooded her shoulders and throat. Stepping out of her trousers, she tried to recall the hundreds of times she'd worn clothes like this in front of television cameras that had sent her picture into millions of homes. That hadn't worried her in the least, so it was foolish to feel as though his eyes could strip her defences and expose her hidden insecurities to the bold light of the sun.

'I'll do your back,' he decreed casually.

Automatically she swivelled, then winced as he poured waterproof sunscreen onto her skin, although the liquid wasn't anywhere near as chilly as it would have been in New Zealand. As his strong fingers spread it across her skin it warmed and softened and sank in.

'There is,' he said, his voice grave, 'reputed to be something extremely seductive about rubbing sunscreen into someone's skin.'

'Really?' Her voice sounded rough-edged; swallowing, she said curtly, 'As Georgia pointed out so vocally yesterday, sunscreen smells and it's sticky. What's seductive about that?'

He didn't laugh but she could hear amusement in his voice. 'Perhaps because rubbing it in gives one licence to notice the intriguing contrast between skin like silk and the muscles beneath.'

Remember, she warned herself again, he's a flirt. You've seen him switch that automatic charm onto every woman he meets.

'And here was I thinking I'd probably lost every tiny bit of muscle tone I might have had,' she said. To her relief, her voice sounded crisp and normal. 'Swimming must be keeping me in reasonable shape.'

'Very reasonable.' He sounded speculative, as though something she'd said had roused his interest.

No, she had to be imagining things.

'Right, that's a couple of hours' worth for you,' he said. His hands smoothed over her shoulder blades and came to rest on her bare shoulders, gripping lightly, the long fingers splayed out over her sensitised skin in a disturbing, unwantedly intimate gesture. Anet felt that touch right through to the soles of her feet. He wasn't standing very close, but he didn't need to; sensation, fiery and untamed, ripped through her.

One of the women looked up at them. Her brows rose and she turned to her companion, saying something in a muted voice.

Anet stepped away, fighting a sudden, hopeless desire to be six inches shorter and considerably lighter. 'Thanks,' she said curtly, holding out her hand for the bottle.

He handed it over. She wanted him to go away—or at least look away—while she slathered the rest of her exposed skin, but he stood and watched her with eyes half closed against the sun's brilliance.

As embarrassed as though she were doing a striptease, yet oddly stimulated by his gaze, she hurried through the process, then ignored the goosebumps on her skin and lifted her voice so that the divers could hear. 'OK, guys, let's see this coral garden.'

Although she'd already explained the hazards to the experienced group, using her inadequate German but relying on their much better English to get her warnings across, she repeated some of the more important warnings.

'You'll get the best photographs within fifteen metres of the top. That's where the fish and corals are, and of course the light is better there too,' she said. Her glance flicked across to a tall man encumbered with an elaborate underwater photography set-up. 'Keep an eye on your watch and your gauges—especially your depth gauge—and on your partner. Watch that drop-off. It's very easy to go down twenty metres without realising it, and if you follow it too far down you risk narcosis. The nearest decompression chamber is in New Zealand; if you get the bends you're going to be damned sick by the time you're stuffed into it.'

They nodded. The tall man with the cameras said seriously, 'I am not foolish. I have photographed the sea all around the world and have not had an accident.'

Reassured, she said, 'Good. But it always pays to be careful. Have fun.'

They fell into the water; both New Zealanders seemed to know what they were doing, so Anet turned to the rest of the group. 'Heavy stuff,' she said, smiling. 'You won't have to worry about narcosis. Stick with me and I'll show you some of the prettiest sights on this planet.'

Not far below the surface of the warm, transparent sea they found the exquisite little denizens of the reef solemnly going about their business like unevenly distributed clusters of highly coloured, mobile jewels. Around them and beneath them the coral spread its variety of shapes and textures and colours, from the delicate fragility of the coral trees to the rounded, solid forms of brain coral.

Anet couldn't enjoy it completely because she had to keep a close eye on her small group, counting heads inconspicuously, checking her contents gauge, until at last she made a gesture and they rose obediently to the surface. For the last time she counted them before leading them back to the boat where Lucas waited.

Deliberately she held back until they were all out,
watching through lashes spiky with salt as he dealt with
them. He was not, she thought with irony as she pulled
herself effortlessly onto the diving platform at the stern,
the sort of man you'd expect to be good at helping
tourists take off fins and scuba gear, but he was, and
they clearly thought he was wonderful.

It had to be those challenging eyes and that killer smile
and the air of—oh, competence? Somehow he exuded
utter reliability. As she towelled her hair dry and pulled
on her T-shirt over her bathing suit she decided that
Lucas was a man who could be trusted to do his best
no matter what the situation.

As well, with him you got the feeling that his best was
going to be better than any other man's.

And that, she told herself, was enough of that. Too
much dwelling on the enigma of Lucas Tremaine was
almost certainly bad for one's mental and emotional
health.

Finger-combing her hair back from her face, she smiled
as she listened to the excited, enraptured comments. She
kept her eyes away from Lucas, but with some subliminal sense noticed the moment he suddenly looked up
and over their heads.

Beyond the flagged buoy a figure was swimming
towards them, arm raised in the air in the classic signal
for help.

Anet and Lucas arrived at the inflatable dinghy at the
same moment. Stooping to snatch up her gear, Anet
realised that Lucas had already grabbed his own.

'Check my gear, will you?' Anet shouted, starting
the outboard in the dinghy. 'Make sure the octopus
valve—'

'Don't be a fool,' he retorted, pulling off his shirt and
checking his own equipment. 'You haven't been up for
ten minutes yet. Even if you had, it would have to be a
limited dive. If you go deep you could get the bends.'

Of course he was right. Biting her lip, Anet sent the little boat flat out across the water to the signalling swimmer, fortunately only a short distance away. Others were appearing on the surface; cursing beneath her breath, she spun the tiller to avoid them.

Somehow she wasn't surprised when the swimmer in trouble turned out to be the black-haired woman from New Zealand, who, as Lucas leaned over to drag her on board, blurted, 'That stupid guy's going down to the drop-off, and he won't take any notice of me. I think he's narced—he was drunk last night so he shouldn't damned well be diving today, but he would come!'

'Where?' Lucas demanded.

'Back where I surfaced.'

Anet had taken a bearing against the land and the motu so she headed towards the spot. In the bow Lucas stood, staring down into the crystal depths.

Pray God he sees him, she thought, and that that fool hasn't gone over the drop-off. Alcohol was well-known for causing swift narcosis; by now he'd be irrational. Her heart clenched as she flashed a glance at Lucas. He looked sure of himself and completely capable of dealing with anything...

Somehow it didn't help.

'Here.' Lucas's voice cracked as hard and fast as a whip. 'I can see him.'

At his first word Anet had cut the engine and turned the tiller, and as soon as the dinghy stopped he slid backwards over the side.

Amidst the swirl of water Anet caught a glimpse of sleek tanned shoulders and long muscular legs, and then there was only a row of bubbles to mark his passage. Helped by the thin-lipped New Zealander, she began to get the extra tanks ready, bracing herself against the round rubber side of the dinghy.

'Is there anything I can do?' asked a heavily accented voice from the water alongside. The photographer.

She said, 'Not here, thanks. Can you go back to the launch and count the others? There should be eight of you.'

'Of course.'

'Thank you,' she said automatically. He headed off towards the boat, calling out to those others who were still in the water.

'Oh, Steve's such a fool,' the woman with her said suddenly. 'He wouldn't take any notice of me at all. I *knew* he shouldn't have dived.'

'You should have told us he'd been on a bender last night,' Anet said neutrally, biting back the words that burned on her tongue. 'I'm sorry, I'm hopeless with names. You're—?'

'Fiona, and you must get so many people on the boat it's a wonder you remember anyone's!'

'Well, Fiona, help me heave these over the side. We'll suspend them at ten feet.'

'I had no idea he was going to pull a stunt like this,' she said gruffly as she moved to assist.

When the bottles had been hung on the anchor rope she said, 'He wouldn't take any notice when I tried to get him to come back. He just kept playing around, getting closer and closer to the drop-off. I was running out of air, and anyway, I thought Lucas might have a better chance of getting him to behave. Steve's a bit of a chauvinist—he doesn't like taking suggestions from women.'

'Lucas knows what he's doing,' Anet said. It was all the reassurance she could give.

Mentally she began to go through the drill for the bends. Speed was of the essence; there was a helicopter on the island, but it was a private one. Still, if it was needed she could call it from the boat and the chopper could pick him up anywhere in the lagoon.

Squinting, she counted the others on the stern of the bigger boat, now crowded with people trying to see what was going on. Yes, it looked as though they were all there, thank heavens. Even as she looked Sule held up her hand, indicating that they were all back. Thank God for that.

Little chills kept chasing each other across her skin, and she felt a familiar hollowness in her stomach. That, however, she had been trained to deal with. Using the relaxation techniques drummed into her by her coach, she began to breathe carefully and evenly, letting her mind settle until the churning edge of panic stilled.

At last she said on a brisk note that probably didn't hide her intense relief, 'Ah, here they are—and your friend is making it on his own, so he's OK.'

'He's only an acquaintance,' Fiona said flatly. 'A diving buddy. But not ever again.'

As the two swimmers pulled themselves in over the side she scanned both faces carefully; the New Zealander looked pale but was obviously all right. Lucas, she realised with a cold, atavistic tremor, was furious.

Once aboard, he spat out his mouthpiece and said dangerously, 'That was a stupid, irresponsible, fool thing to do.'

Steve said, 'Look, I'm an experienced diver—'

'You were narced,' Lucas said, his voice icily quiet.

'Hell, I didn't go below thirty metres. I wasn't even down that far when you bloody jerked me off the floor—and I had plenty of air left.'

'You didn't stick to the dive plan. You were fiddling around near the drop-off when everyone else had started to come back up, and I had to manhandle you off the bottom. I'll bet you were as high as a kite.'

'I knew what I was doing!'

Completely unimpressed, Lucas said, 'Then why did I have to hold you at ten feet? You can drown off someone else's boat, not this one—it's bad for business.'

He blustered, 'I've dived all over the world—deep dives—'

'If you were drunk last night,' Anet said curtly, 'you damned well shouldn't have been diving today.'

Steve gave Fiona a filthy look. Unimpressed, she said, 'Face it, Steve, you were stupid and you know it.'

Lucas said brutally, 'Keep up stunts like today's and you'll be dead in a year.' Ignoring Anet's nod, he went on, 'Don't ever pull a stunt like that off a commercial diving boat again.'

With an ugly, belligerent glare at his companion, the other man retorted, 'Nobody asked you to—'

'Save you from drowning?' Lucas interposed in a tone that could have flayed the hide from a shark.

'I was not bloody drowning!' Glowering at Fiona, he demanded, 'What the hell do you think you were doing, you stupid bitch? I don't need a nursemaid—'

'That,' Lucas said, the silky words lifting the hairs on the back of Anet's neck, 'is enough of that.' He paused, looking at Steve's clenched fists. 'You'll shut up and behave yourself or I'll have you in a prison cell so fast you won't see the way we go, and you'll stay there until they put you on the first flight out. The authorities here do not like troublemakers.'

'You can't do that!'

'I can.' His cold confidence silenced the other man. Speaking clearly and contemptuously, Lucas continued, 'You might think it's fun to play ducks and drakes with your body, but capers like today's endanger others.'

'Bloody hell, what a fuss about nothing!' Steve summoned truculence to overlay the instinctive fear of the weak faced with the strong. 'I know what I'm doing! I wasn't in any danger, damn you!'

'Then you must have gills,' Luke said flatly, 'as well as a brain the size of a flatfish's.' He cut short the other man's curse. 'Watch your mouth.' There wasn't any appreciable expression on his face or in his tone, but the none too subtle menace he projected had its effect.

Steve looked from one to the other, then sneered, 'God, if I'd known there was going to be all this carry-on I wouldn't have gone more than ten feet under. It isn't worth the hassle.'

Lucas said with negligent scorn, 'All the men I've known who thought it macho and heroic and clever to dive deeply are dead. And anyone who fiddles around with narcosis is going to die sooner rather than later. The first sign is euphoria—the same feeling drunkenness gives you.' Without waiting for a response, as though insultingly certain that nothing he could say would penetrate such stupidity, he nodded at Anet. 'Let's get back to the boat.'

Later, when Anet took Lucas a can of mineral water while he brought them in through the gap of the reef, he commented, 'You can certainly handle that dinghy.'

Absurdly pleased by such a small compliment, she shrugged. 'I've been in and around the water most of my life. I learned to row before I could walk, just about. Do you think that guy will take any notice of what you said?'

'Probably not,' he said indifferently.

He'd put his shirt back on, but Anet recalled the width and power of his shoulders beneath it and looked away, something clenching in the pit of her stomach.

She said, 'He'll kill himself.'

'Life's cruel to the stupid.' He drank from the can, the muscles working in his tanned throat.

'Well, if he does drown at least it won't be from Scott's boat.'

'Nor on Fala'isi,' Lucas said with a certain cold satisfaction. 'I'll spread the word.'

She looked at him. 'Can you do that?'

'Oh, yes. I'll contact a friend tonight. No one else will accept him for a diving trip while he's on the island.'

By the time the sun slid languidly towards the horizon Anet was more tired than she'd been even during her first few exhausting days. That Lucas had been a distinct hit with both the morning divers and the afternoon snorkellers did not make her feel any better.

That, of course, was only to be expected among the female clients, but Anet had been surprised to see the

way men had reacted to him. Perhaps it was his size, she
thought as the boat headed across the lagoon towards
the little town. Lean, tanned hands on the wheel, Lucas
stood in the wheelhouse talking to a couple of men. They
were big, but Lucas was bigger, and he seemed to vibrate
with a compelling masculine charisma that captured attention without seeking it.

Body language revealed all. Although Lucas appeared
relaxed, something in the way he stood, the way he
moved, indicated complete control over both himself and
the situation. Searching for a word to describe him, she
could only come up again with competent, which was
so much less than what she meant.

He looked to be the master of his life. Not un-
breakable—no, he was human and therefore at the mercy
of fate, as his wife's death had shown—but if anyone
could mould destiny and subvert it, it would be Lucas
Tremaine.

As Steve had so reluctantly, the two men with him
responded to his inbuilt authority. There was respect in
the way they stood, the way they spoke to him. They
weren't overtly deferential, and yet—body language
again!—they recognised the power of the man and knew
that it was greater than theirs.

We're still a primitive species, she thought. Strength
is important, physical strength as well as mental. Men
who had both were highly rated.

'Lucky you,' a woman murmured from beside her.

Heat rose through Anet's skin. It was embarrassing
to be caught staring at him like some lovesick idiot.

Especially as honesty compelled her to admit, 'He's
not mine.'

'So he's a free agent?'

A twinge of something—surely not jealousy?—un-
settled her. 'As far as I know,' she said cheerfully, turning
to smile at the woman, a pleasantly attractive American
wearing her thirty-five or so years with the smooth

sophistication and confidence that seemed to be a national characteristic.

'But you wish he weren't,' the woman said shrewdly.

'I only met him yesterday,' Anet told her, not attempting to hide the dry note in her voice.

The American laughed. 'I married my first husband three weeks after we met, and we were idyllically happy— I was probably happier than I've ever been since. He died five years later, so I don't know whether it would have lasted, but I'm glad we had those years.'

'I'll bet you are,' Anet said, something in the other woman's words striking a chord of sympathy. 'How are you enjoying Fala'isi?'

'Oh, it's glorious!'

Ten minutes later, after listening to a rhapsody about the island, Anet was called away to attend to a woman who felt faint. When next she looked up it was to see the American talking to Lucas, her animated expression and low, husky laughter indicating how very interesting she found him.

For some obscure reason it hurt. Anet's wide shoulders lifted slightly before she got on with her work, but the image of them together nagged in her brain.

She was relieved when at last they had finished—later then usual because Lucas was even more fussy about checking the gear than Scott had been and they'd found a couple of straps that needed replacement.

Then the dive bottles had to be loaded onto the truck and taken off to be refilled at the depot. Tomorrow morning they'd go over each one with the gauge again, but for today work was over. Anet walked beside Lucas in the dusty hindside of afternoon as the sun prepared for its rapid descent into the sea. The little town hummed all day and into the night, but there was a hiatus—'gin time' Scott called it—when people sat down and talked as they gathered strength for the night ahead.

Self-conscious at the silence, Anet said, 'I don't think we've forgotten anything.'

'Oh, we probably have, but the day went off well.'

'Thanks to you. That unmitigated fool must have thought he was related to Neptune. Did you have much trouble with him?'

'I damned near had to haul him up by his neck.' Lucas's voice was sardonic. 'And hold him still on the stops.'

Anet felt ill. He was certainly strong enough to deal with the New Zealander, but there was always danger in dealing with a diver confused by narcosis. Sternly recalling what she had planned to say, she persevered, 'I should have gone down.'

'Don't be silly.'

'I mean it. You shouldn't have risked your life—'

'Anet, you couldn't go back. Surely you know that you've got to be up for ten minutes,' he said curtly.

'By the time you took off I'd had ten minutes. And Scott is my relative.'

He looked down his long nose at her, his eyes quizzical and aloof. 'And what has that got to do with anything?'

'Just that—you're doing Scott a favour. He'd feel like hell if anything happened to you.'

He gave her a cynical smile. 'Don't worry, Anet, no one is going to come demanding accountability from Scott. I'm a free agent.'

No self-pity corroded his deep voice, nothing but sardonic amusement, yet she felt a pang of compassion. She said gruffly, 'I'm the one with the instructor's certificate.'

'I have one too,' he said calmly.

'That's not the point. I—'

'Apart from anything else, I went after him because he was a big man,' he interrupted. 'I thought I would be better able to deal with him. And he was also the sort who'd refuse to take orders from a woman.'

'I'm surprised you remembered which one he was.'

'I'm a writer; I watch people. I remembered him because Fiona was his buddy.' They stopped by Scott's car and he bent and slipped the key into the lock. 'And she had hair like Cara's—my wife's,' he said casually.

Smooth and flowing down across her shoulders, a fall of ebony glowing with blue highlights. Anet fell silent, not realising until they were almost back home that he had neatly sidestepped her original complaint.

It couldn't have been deliberate, could it? No, no man was cold-blooded enough to use his dead wife's name to stop an argument.

With relief, she gave up such questions for practicalities. 'You'll have to sleep in Scott and Serena's room. I don't know whether there's any spare space in the wardrobe—'

'I'm accustomed to living out of a suitcase,' he said negligently. 'Don't worry about it.'

CHAPTER FIVE

SHE did, however. While he spoke on the telephone, clearly altering plans, she changed the sheets on Scott and Serena's bed and got a towel, then looked for a moment around the fairly spartan room. It was comfortable, but nowhere near as luxurious as the hotel he'd been staying in.

Catching sight of herself in the mirror, she grimaced. Salt had left its stains on her face, and her hair was lank against her head. More than anything she needed to wash off the sunscreen and sweat.

Collecting her dressing-gown, she headed into the bathroom, where she showered as quickly as she could. Not quickly enough, however. As she emerged Lucas turned the corner into the hall.

'Your room's through that door,' she said, trying to convince herself that her blue and white seersucker robe was a perfectly adequate cover. 'And the bathroom's clear. Oh—what about your clothes?'

'They've just arrived,' he said. 'Where are the sheets and linen kept?'

'I've remade the bed and put a towel on the end of it.'

He smiled, and once more her stomach performed a sudden leap.

'Thank you,' he said.

Safely in her own room, she decided that from now on she'd take her clothes into the bathroom. It would mean they'd get damp—the air-conditioning unit was overworked—but at least she wouldn't have to worry about meeting him in the hall again wearing only her dressing-gown.

Which was stupid; he hadn't been in the least interested in her, even though the cloth had been moulded to her damp skin.

And that, she admitted with enormous, painful reluctance, was what hurt.

The closing of the bathroom door and the muted hum of the fan stopped that train of thought, replacing it with another, even more uncomfortable one. She had watched with awed fascination as he'd stripped off his shirt, and the memory of that sleek skin, golden in the tropical sun, gleaming with the sheen of perfect health, was still far too clear in her mind.

He had been overwhelming, and Anet had seen enough athletes at the peak of their condition to be not easily overwhelmed.

Banishing such dangerous images, she dithered for a while trying to choose suitable clothes for an evening with Lucas. They hadn't organised dinner, which meant they'd probably have to rustle something up from the fridge, so the most practical choice would be a T-shirt over cotton trousers. However, without actually making a decision, she took down a silk shirt she was particularly fond of.

The fan was still going in the bathroom when she emerged. She could even hear the faint hiss of the shower. Firmly disciplining her over-active imagination, she headed for the small kitchen and peered into the depths of the fridge, frowning as she noted the food there.

It would have to be risotto with a salad, which hardly seemed enough for a man of Lucas's size, even eked out with ice-cream and fruit. She should have bought a fish down at the docks. Ah, well, she could do that tomorrow.

It might not be a good idea to put the rice on just yet, in case he preferred to eat much later. Swallowing to ease a dry throat, she realised that she could do with a cup of tea, so filled the kettle and plugged it in.

After hesitating absurdly for a moment she went into the sitting room and looked along the shelves. Yes, there were Lucas's books. She pulled his latest one out, but before she had a chance to do more than glance at the cover a noise in the hall made her stuff it hastily back. Feeling foolish—for why should it matter if he found her looking at his work?—she hurried across the room to the window and stared through the glass at the frilled scarlet flowers on a hibiscus shrub.

Endeavouring to appear cool and collected, she raised her eyes enquiringly as he came into the room, and suddenly her mouth went from dry to unbearably parched. Wearing trousers, and with a towel slung around his shoulders and a few beads of moisture emphasising the gleaming contours of his chest, he seemed the epitome of maleness—too big, too overpowering, almost lethal in his sexual splendour.

'We should go out to dinner,' he said.

'That would be nice, but we're not going to meet many new customers at dinner,' she said, holding her voice steady with an effort. 'I think Scott finds the nightclubs a more profitable hunting ground.'

His smile was a nice blend of irony and understanding. 'I don't intend to drum up custom,' he said coolly. 'Apart from anything else, the only place I plan to wear that T-shirt is out on the boat.'

A stock of suitably inscribed hats and shirts and shorts was kept for sale on the diving launch; only one T-shirt had fitted Lucas. It should have looked ridiculous on him, but it hadn't. His uncompromising, almost arrogant authority had transcended the inherent tackiness of the advertising.

'Not many men are as big as you are,' Sule had murmured as he'd tried it on just before the customers arrived.

He'd given her that automatic charming smile, and when he'd left the cabin Sule had grinned and rolled her eyes at Anet. 'I hope he decides to stay here,' she'd said. Anet had learned that you could laugh when you were feeling angry and outraged and edgy.

Now she said, 'Scott wouldn't expect you to.'

'I'll do a lot for Scott, but not that. Tonight's dinner will be a small celebration because we got through our first day without any mishaps.'

A fragile bubble of anticipation expanded in her chest. 'Sounds fun. Where do you think we should go?'

'Samulele's.'

It was the most expensive restaurant on Fala'isi. She surveyed her trousers, saying, 'I don't think I've anything suitable to wear.'

'Of course you have,' he said calmly. 'What you've got on is fine.'

Her head came up sharply. He was eyeing her with bland composure, so apparently he really thought that black trousers and a floaty black and gold shirt enlivened with touches of aquamarine were suitable to wear to a restaurant which had been reviewed by a London critic as 'one of the best in the South Pacific—no, in the world!'

It would have to do; she had nothing else. 'You might have difficulty getting a table,' she observed.

'I already have one.'

Of course.

She said, 'When are we due?'

He didn't look at his watch. Did he always know the time—by osmosis?—or didn't he care? Probably the latter; his splendid self-sufficiency would free him from the tyranny of worrying about what people thought.

'In half an hour,' he said. 'I thought it better to make it early. We've had an exhausting day.'

She had, but she was prepared to bet that he was no more weary than he had been at seven that morning. And hers was more a tiredness of the spirit than of the body.

Anet distrusted his ability to see past the mask she presented to the world. Those turquoise eyes missed very little—as he'd told her, he was a writer, and people were his trade. Besides, he'd spent years investigating dangerous causes in places where keen eyes and quick perception might well make the difference between life and death.

'Good idea,' she said, keeping her gaze away from the row of books on the shelf. Thinking of the risks he'd taken to gather the information in them made her feel ill. 'I'm making a pot of tea. Would you like a cup?'

'I'll have a beer, thanks,' he said.

Half an hour later as they drove through the quiet, palm-guarded streets, she said, 'When I first came to the tropics I was really surprised to see suburbs. Somehow I'd expected it to be quite different from the rest of the world.'

'Huts made of pandanus and banana leaves set on pristine white beaches backed by coconut palms?'

She smiled. 'There are places like that.'

'They're getting to be fewer and fewer. Fala'isi is one of the rare places where islanders still live in their villages. Expatriates live in these streets.'

'I know. I really like roads lined with poincianas and frangipani and kapok trees, but it's suburbia just the same. We westerners carry our civilisation with us on our backs.'

His broad shoulders lifted. 'That's what the world will be like in a hundred years, unless something happens to stop it.'

She asked, 'Is that why you sail round the Pacific?'

His teeth were white in his tanned face. 'I suppose so. To enjoy the secret, beautiful places before it's too late.'

'And yet,' she said slowly, 'it's not fair to keep people in a museum because they're more satisfying to tourists there.'

'It can't be done. Only sentimentalists yearn for the past.'

'Which might look pretty to us now,' she said crisply, 'but had its flaws.'

'Everything has flaws.' His voice was cool, his tone oddly oblique. 'Just as well, because I don't think we're built to cope with perfection. If we find it by chance we ruin it as quickly as we can.'

He certainly wasn't sentimental.

Anet would have liked to probe further, but something about the set of his shoulders, the detachment in his voice, warned her not to trespass.

The restaurant was organised into a series of rooms separated by screens of foliage and half-walls of plaited pandanus. Although there was a distinct tropical ambience, it was sophisticated, far from the rustic atmosphere of the club the night before, yet inspired by the magic and transcendental beauty of the South Sea islands.

Huge arrangements of exotic flowers topped elegant ceramic pots, and as Anet walked past one she noticed that a spike of torch ginger had a small brown and green gecko sprawled out along its stem, its unblinking eyes watching for a passing insect.

'This is lovely,' she said after they'd been seated.

Lucas smiled. 'It's very clever,' he responded. 'Just what the well-heeled tourist wants: atmosphere without any of the discomforts.'

'Are you as much a cynic as you seem to be?'

'Oh, yes,' he returned, his eyes cold and hard and opaque. 'And don't be fooled by whichever idiot it was who said a cynic was a wounded romantic. I'm not romantic at all. Are you, Anet?'

The waiter came up then with the menus, so she was able to avoid answering his question. However, when they had ordered he asked it again.

'No,' she said easily. 'I'm basically practical and down-to-earth. I do whatever has to be done.'

His eyes flicked to the hand she'd curved around the cool stem of her wine glass. He had ordered a New Zealand *méthode champenoise,* well chilled and with a hint of fruitiness that made it ideal as an aperitif.

'Yet you have the long fingers of an idealist,' he said.

'So do you,' she retorted. 'Surely you don't believe that fingers reveal character?'

'Of course I don't. The conventions, however, are hard to resist. Full lips indicate a sensuous temperament, thin lips meanness. A big person is clumsy. Eyes set close together show that one can't be trusted. How many characters have been warped by people's expectations of them, even if the expectations are unspoken, almost unrecognised?'

It was something Anet had never thought of before. Intrigued, she leaned forward. 'I suppose it does happen when you first meet a person—we carry all sorts of baggage with us—but surely as one gets to know new acquaintances those assumptions go down the drain?'

At the edge of her sight a subdued ripple of motion transformed itself into a woman—no, two women. Anet met the green gaze of Georgia Sanderson, accompanied again by Penny. Georgia, it seemed, had nosed out the one place on the island that had an international reputation.

'Hello!' she said, stopping with a flourish, her eyes gleaming with interest and something else. 'Fancy seeing you here!'

Smiling, Lucas got to his feet, which left Anet in the uncomfortable position of being the only person sitting, so she too rose. Her height, she thought mordantly as she looked down on the latest arrivals, did occasionally come in handy.

'Penny and I decided to see what Fala'isi can do with *haute cuisine*,' Georgia said vivaciously, speaking, Anet was ridiculously pleased to hear, with an atrocious French accent. She turned to Anet, widened her eyes and said, 'You must have thought me a total idiot yesterday.'

Anet said, 'Oh, no, lots of people simply don't realise how dangerous the sun can be—'

A delighted trill of laughter interrupted her. 'No, no, not that. I didn't recognise you! Jan has never told me that her sister is a world-famous javelin-thrower. It wasn't until we were having a nightcap that someone told me all about you!'

Had she stressed the last few words? Anet didn't dare look at Lucas, but she felt his attention like a weight on her soul.

Her tormentor continued sweetly, 'Of course, I should have known who you were, but I'm afraid I don't watch field sports very much, and I certainly don't read the tabloids.'

Anet swallowed. There could be no doubt what she was referring to; the newspaper that had carried the story branding her a kidnapper had been a British tabloid. She wanted to say something but her tongue felt thick and heavy in her mouth, and her brain had turned to custard.

After allowing the silence to stretch to a disquieting length, Georgia went on, 'As far as sport goes, gymnastics and diving are about the limits of my interest—they're so graceful and clever. But I felt a perfect nitwit when I was told who you were—especially as I did think your face looked vaguely familiar.'

Anet forced her clumsy mind to summon words. 'There is nothing less interesting than yesterday's sportsperson.' She flashed a glance at Lucas, saw his face, set and still, his eyes gleaming beneath his thick lashes. From somewhere she found the strength to say, 'But Lucas is far more famous than I ever was. He's a writer.'

'I know,' Georgia purred. 'We discussed your books yesterday, didn't we, Lucas? I found them utterly absorbing. Every one a bestseller—and rightly so. They're brilliant!' She gave him a commiserating smile. 'If you were an American you'd have won the Pulitzer Prize several times over.'

It was impossible to tell what he thought of such fulsome appreciation. 'Thank you,' he said gravely.

Georgia tilted her head a little to smile at him, a conspiratorial smile that shut out everyone else, before murmuring, 'Well, we'd better be on our way, I suppose.

Come on, Penny.' And she followed the patient waiter
into the further reaches of the restaurant—out of sight,
Anet was pleased to see.

'Are you all right?' Lucas asked as they sat down
again.

'I'm fine,' she replied. But her voice sounded hollow,
and she thought he looked sharply at her.

All he said, however, was, 'What would you like to
eat?'

Picking up the menu, she perused it before saying
vaguely, 'Fish, I think. They have superb fish here.'

'We have superb fish in New Zealand too.'

'I know, but they're different fish.'

He nodded as though she'd made sense. 'What about
an entrée?'

No doubt Georgia toyed with salads all night long.
Anet said firmly, 'I'll have the iced avocado soup, then
the fish baked in gin.'

'Gin?'

Solemnly she replied, 'It's an old Polynesian recipe.'

His eyebrows rose. 'The Polynesians didn't have
juniper trees. Thus, they couldn't have had gin.'

'Well, Sule did say that it came from Tahiti,' she said.
'Perhaps the French introduced it.'

'I don't think gin is a particularly French drink. More
likely Captain Cook and his crew of bemused sailors
had something to do with it.'

The waiter reappeared and Lucas ordered the meal;
he chose, Anet noted with an odd and highly suspect
little glow of pleasure, the same as she had.

Then he picked up his wine glass and drank with appreciation but no reverence before asking with idle
interest, 'What made you decide to become a
physiotherapist?'

'My grandmother used to suffer from a bad back, and
the only thing that gave her any relief was physiotherapy. And of course while I was competing I saw the
kind of miracles a good physio can work.'

'I see,' he said.

Anet's shoulders moved slightly; she had the uncomfortable feeling that he really did see—far more than she wanted him to.

'Did you always intend making it your career?'

Was he probing? Looking down at her fingers, she chose her words with caution. 'Yes. Sport got in the way for a while, but I knew that however well I did at the Olympics I was going to give it up afterwards. I just wanted to do the best I could. Both the gold and the world record were added extras—wonderful bonuses. Once it was over I found that the driving need was gone. I wanted to live real life for a change. It's only sport,' she said, and tried for a smile. 'Nothing world-shaking, just a search for individual excellence and therefore rather selfish. My coach would kill me for saying that, but it's true.'

That statement surprised him. His eyes were very shrewd as he said, 'So you gave it all up—the cheers and the tension and the adulation, testing yourself every day, the breathless concentration before the first throw and the elation when you'd pushed yourself that little bit further.'

His preception startled her in turn. 'You seem to know all about it.'

'It's not too difficult to imagine what it must be like to be an athlete.' His mouth curved into a smile with more than a tinge of mockery to it. 'I get something of the same feeling when I start a book. Tell me, did the steroid scandal have anything to do with your decision to retire?'

Disappointment speared through her, mixed with a chagrin so keen it almost made her wince. To give herself time to think, she picked up her glass, but set it down without taking more than a token sip. He watched each movement as though he understood the half-formed thoughts that led to it. Careful, she told herself. Lucas

Tremaine has dealt with liars far more experienced than you are.

'A little,' she admitted.

He nodded. 'But you were clean. And your sporting body came out heavily in your favour when Victoria Sutter accused you of taking steroids before the Olympics.'

'I know.'

'Do you think she took steroids?' he asked indolently.

Without thinking she sipped some more wine, feeling the bubbles break softly as the liquid slid over her tongue. 'She tested clear too,' she said as she set the glass down.

'You don't sound entirely satisfied.'

'She tested clear,' she repeated. 'I had to be satisfied.'

He said evenly, unsparingly, 'And then she was kidnapped and removed from the scene during the run-up to the Games. Kidnapped, she later said, by you. Although of course she had no real proof.'

So there it was, right out in the open.

Forcing herself to set aside the stupid sense of betrayal that iced through her, she selected words with precision, banishing remembered anger and frustration from her voice so that she sounded judicial and objective. 'She wasn't exactly herself when she made those accusations.'

He said mildly, 'I suppose her allegations in the Press were a complete surprise to you?'

'She told me on the first day of the Games that if I beat her she'd go to the newspapers with her story.'

Convinced that her allegations were the result of 'roid rage'—the senseless fury that came from the use of steroids—Anet had tried to ignore her. However, no sooner had the Games finished than the newspaper had printed the story.

It had been a bitter time for Anet. Dogged by reporters and questioned by police, she had fought grimly for her reputation, all along knowing that she was going to retire, and that her retirement would be taken as a sign of guilt.

'She never competed again, did she?' Lucas asked with lazy persistence.

Anet said steadily, 'No, she didn't. I don't know what happened to her.'

'And you don't care.'

His voice was level, without inflection, yet an equivocal undernote brought her head up swiftly. He met her gaze with coolly enquiring eyes.

Colour leached from her skin as she said with a sudden fierce emphasis, 'Not particularly.'

'Did she tell the newspaper that you had organised her kidnapping?'

'The newspaper refused to reveal its source,' she said tonelessly, but was unable to stop herself from adding, 'However, it printed a retraction as soon as she went underground.'

'Wasn't anyone concerned when she disappeared? Didn't anyone worry—especially in light of her claim to have been kidnapped before?'

Unease screwed up her nerves unbearably. Although his voice was as aloof, as unemotional as hers, she sensed an unwavering purpose beneath the controlled detachment. This, she thought wearily, was how the people he interviewed for his books must feel—harried and driven and angry, with a sick panic clouding their mind and shredding their judgement.

She said, 'I'm afraid I was too angry with her to worry.'

'She'd made her bed—let her lie in it?' he suggested. When she remained silent he asked, 'Why did she hate you?'

The question took her by surprise, so that before she had a chance to reconsider she responded indiscreetly, 'She thought I stole her sponsorship money.'

'And did you?'

Anet's mouth firmed. 'No,' she said.

'I seem to remember you representing a bank,' he said.

She said remotely, 'I didn't take any sponsorship money. I didn't need it.'

'Ah, yes, of course. You're an heiress.'

She sent him a coldly measuring glance. 'I have a rich father, who supported me,' she said. 'And my grand-mother left me a small legacy. If that's being an heiress, then I suppose I am.'

He smiled. 'It all depends on what you call small,' he said. 'I imagine Victoria considered you to be rich.'

'Victoria got sponsorship easily,' she said flatly. 'She was so beautiful and photogenic that she had firms and organisations falling over themselves to sign her up. Un-fortunately she didn't seem to be able to understand that sponsors want an athlete who can be relied on to turn up when she's told to—someone good-humoured and pleasant, especially to the media and the public.

'She started to believe her publicity—that "Venus of the South Seas" bit went to her head—and she got ar-rogant. I filled in for her a couple of times, and then the firm that was sponsoring her dumped her. The ath-letics association asked me to take over the contract be-cause they needed the publicity. So I did. And I gave the sponsorship money to the association.'

'She must have been desperate. What did she do?'

Anet's skin crawled. Victoria had told her she'd slept with men for payment so that she could keep going; she had flung the fact at Anet, sneering at Anet's horror and saying wildly, 'You forced me to do it, you sancti-monious bitch!'

Knowing that whatever she said now was going to sound heartless, Anet said, 'She had the guts to claw her way off the floor after a childhood that would have sent most of us into permanent psychosis. She managed somehow.'

'But she blamed you?' he said, eyes keenly perceptive beneath his thick lashes.

She shrugged. 'She thought—or pretended to think— that I'd been scheming behind her back. She believed that the reason I was offered the sponsorship in her place was because I had connections.'

'What was she like?' he asked.

Lifting her chin, she said evenly, 'I found her—and so did almost everyone else who came across her—infuriating, abrasive and underhand; on occasions she could be downright dishonest. But that was just Victoria. There are plenty of egos in the sporting world, and some extremely difficult people. I never—'

'You never?' he prompted.

'I didn't wish her any harm,' she said. 'I didn't even care about beating her in particular. I was just determined to do the best I could.'

It was Victoria who'd made the competition personal, Victoria who'd wanted that gold medal with an obsessiveness that had bordered on the unhealthy. Although Anet could understand that her actions had been based on a deep-rooted insecurity, it hadn't made them easier to bear.

At that moment, thank heavens, the waiter appeared with the first course. Lucas stopped talking as the plates were set down carefully, and more wine was poured before the man disappeared. Her stomach roiling, Anet stared at the smooth pale green soup with distaste before picking up her spoon.

Why was she discussing all this with a man she had met only the previous day? Although her coach had helped her deal with Victoria's naked antagonism, she had never spoken of it to anyone else except her father.

Abruptly she asked, 'Why are you interested in this old story anyway?'

'Curiosity, I'm afraid,' he said unhurriedly. 'I knew of the rumours, of course—knew that you had forced that English rag to print a retraction. I heard your father called in some very heavy artillery.'

'He believed me,' she said. A niggling and very unwise impulse of self-pity goaded her to add, 'But it didn't make any difference. Ask anyone in this world today

what happened, and most of them will say that where
there's smoke there's fire, and that probably I did ar-
range to have Victoria Sutter kidnapped. So in a way
she won.'

'Hardly,' he said, his tone satirical. 'She's dropped
completely out of sight, whereas you're obviously happy,
you have a profession you enjoy and you appear to have
the best that life can offer.'

Anet responded too quickly to the note of cynicism
she thought she detected in his voice. 'I don't believe in
dwelling in the past.'

'Yet you're still very prickly about the whole business,'
he observed, watching her with narrowed eyes.

Dipping her spoon into the soup, she used the small
action as a reason to avoid looking at him. 'Surely that's
natural,' she said after a few moments. 'It was the most
exciting moment of my life, followed within days by the
worst. I remember the turmoil rather than the pleasure.
Your colleagues can be utterly terrifying when they roam
in packs.'

'Your ambivalence is understandable,' he said drily.
'Still, looked at with a cool and logical eye, you certainly didn't come out the loser.'

'I only lost my reputation, and what's that?' she
agreed, summoning her sweetest smile. '*You* aren't sure,
are you? You think that I might have done it.'

He surveyed her face with narrowed, unsparing eyes.
'I did read an article where you said that the most important thing in your life was that gold medal.'

Her mouth compressed. 'Ever been misquoted?'

'Occasionally.' But he didn't believe her.

Her smile felt clumsy and painful and crooked. 'So
there you are,' she said, and lifted her spoon to her
mouth.

The soup was smooth and cool and it slid down her
parched throat, which was all she needed from it. Just
as well, because she didn't actually taste a drop.

She wanted him to accept her innocence, and the intensity and passion of that longing terrified her. His opinion meant too much, and she was far too aware of him. As well as a presence that sent small, hot shivers of sensation through her, Lucas possessed an enigmatic self-sufficiency that was at once a threat and a challenge. Add to that intelligence and competence, and he was dangerous.

She would, she decided, re-read his books and see what she could garner from them. Perhaps a mean streak would come through, a pettiness she could safely despise.

Given time and willpower, her weakness for tall, authoritative men could be overcome. And willpower was something she had plenty of. It had got her to the pinnacle of her sporting career then helped her through the anger and frustration of the following months, and it was going to see her through this temporary aberration. Perhaps she should treat the situation as an exercise and begin visualising herself, heart-whole and cheerful, watching Lucas sail away.

'I wonder what's going through your mind,' he said lazily.

She froze, then produced a smile. 'I was thinking that willpower—determination—is an important quality.'

He watched her with brilliant, half-closed eyes. 'Very. Of course too much—or wrongly directed—and it can be dangerous.'

'So can anything,' she retorted.

Leaning back in his chair, he asked drily, 'Compassion?'

'If it becomes over-protective and debilitating.'

'You're a hard woman.' A smile failed to take the sting from the words.

'Possibly.' She wasn't going to let him get away with that. 'Any emotion or attribute can become dangerous if it's allowed free rein. Even too much common sense can deprive a life of excitement and joy.'

'So you don't believe in allowing—to take a purely hypothetical situation—a grand passion free rein?'

She hesitated, conscious that beneath the amused tone and slight mockery there was something else. 'No,' she said cautiously. 'I think it's very easy to say "But I was overwhelmed. I had to. I just couldn't resist it." The problem with that sort of thinking and behaviour is that people don't accept responsibility for their own actions.'

'And that is important?'

'To me it is.'

The waiter returned to lovingly set a spray of frangipani straight in its crystal vase, sending a breath of sweet, exotic perfume across the white tablecloth. Beaming at them both, he removed the soup plates. His presence provided Anet with a moment's breathing space. She was seized by a suspicion that she was giving important information away, and, ridiculous though such a feeling was, she couldn't shake it off.

When the man had gone Lucas said, 'So you always accept the results of your own actions?'

She allowed herself a small ironic smile. 'Sometimes I might not like it,' she said, 'but I hope I do.'

She thought she saw a gleam of satisfaction trapped for a moment in his gaze, and was startled at her response to it—a shudder of deep-seated fear, surely as baseless as it was violent?

Stop being an idiot, she thought exasperatedly; you're behaving like an overheated kettle, ready to blow for no apparent reason.

The delicate image in the miniature Olivia had sent her flashed into her mind. That young woman, she thought with mordant humour, certainly wouldn't have let herself get into such a tizz over a mere man! Like Jan, like their mother, she'd have known instinctively from the cradle how to manage the men in her life.

Anet looked down at her plate. She doubted very much whether Lucas Tremaine would allow himself to be managed by anyone—even a woman as skilled in the art of pleasing men as her sister.

She said, 'Not that I think we make our own lives entirely. There are some things you can't avoid. I admit to bad luck, misfortune—call it what you like.'

'Well, yes, I rather think you should,' he said, an unsettling note rasping through the deep voice.

Too late, she remembered that his wife had died because of his actions. 'I didn't mean to sound arrogant,' she agreed hastily. 'Bad luck exists, but I think *we* decide how to deal with it; we make our own lives, we decide whether to be happy or unhappy, achievers or failures.' And immediately felt that she should have stopped after the first sentence.

'It's a nice, simplistic, New Age outlook,' he said crisply. 'You don't accept that character traits can be inherited, and that therefore life might be more difficult for some than for others?'

'To a certain extent I do, but I refuse to believe that we're born predestined to become one thing or another. I think that's a cop-out.'

'Ah, but the latest research tells us that we may very well be just that. Our happiness probably does lie in our genes.'

They spent the rest of the meal discussing this; he was interesting and he listened carefully, as no other person had except her father and her coach. He also revealed a wide knowledge of the latest scientific theories, which he was able to explain without sounding condescending. Clear and concise, his every sentence revealed a formidable, incisive intellect.

Anet could have dealt with a purely superficial attraction, but the mind behind the splendid body and classically sculpted features was rapidly becoming a fascinating challenge. And although she enjoyed herself very much she became more and more alarmed by the helpless nature of her response to him.

Eventually she excused herself and found the cloakroom. She was almost ready to emerge from her cubicle when she heard the door open and two women come in. Somehow it seemed inevitable that she hear Georgia's voice. But it was what she said as they came in through the door that froze Anet into place.

'How the hell does she do it, the fat cow? The most magnificent hunk I've seen on this grotty little island and she manages to glue herself to him.'

'Perhaps he's sorry for her,' Penny suggested.

'Men are not usually sorry for great tubs of lard! Did you *see* the way she stuffed herself at lunch yesterday? That slab of cheesecake she demolished was big enough to pave a patio.'

Penny laughed. 'You're cross because you lusted after that cheesecake and wouldn't let yourself have any because it was too fattening. Anyway, you're letting envy cloud your judgement. She's big-boned and muscly and tall, but she's not fat.'

'You're so *sweet* when you're trying to be kind,' Georgia cooed. 'Whatever, she's totally unfeminine.'

'And therefore no competition,' the second woman returned.

They both laughed, as though the idea of Anet being competition was so *outré* as to be exquisitely amusing.

It was not the first time Anet had been on the receiving end of such comments. The old cringe returned in full force, was banished. These two were not being deliberately cruel; they didn't know she was there. Anyway, although their cattiness hurt, she didn't care what anyone else thought of her. She knew her own worth.

'Well, I certainly made her sit up this evening,' Georgia said with satisfaction.

'Just so long as you don't drag me into it,' Penny returned a little curtly.

'What do you mean?'

'You know exactly what I mean. "It wasn't until we were having a nightcap that someone told me all about you",' she quoted. 'I thought you were going to spit out everything I told you.'

'So did she,' Georgia said smugly. 'It really rattled her.'

'I know you don't like Jan, but what's poor Anet done to get up your nose so badly?'

'She reminds me of one of my schoolmistresses. Anet has the same look in her eyes. "We can't take responsibility for you unless you apply sunscreen",' she mimicked savagely. 'So hatefully smug—"Do this because I'm bigger than you are, and I have the power here, and I hate women who are smaller than me who have the total and damned audacity to be attractive to men when I am not." I can't help it if I have enough self-control not to feed my face every time I go past a table.'

'G, be fair—she had to say that. It'd be bad for business if you grilled yourself to a crisp.'

'She did her best to make me look a fool. I suppose that bitch Jan's been slagging me off.'

'Well, you slag her off at every available opportunity. Even if she has, who cares?'

There was silence for several moments. Anet wished she had the courage to walk out of the cubicle and face them down, but like a coward she stayed there, hardly daring to breathe in case they realised she was there.

Then Georgia said thoughtfully, 'Do you think she did it? Kidnapped that woman?'

CHAPTER SIX

'How should I know? But I doubt it—no one else seems to think so.'

'Hah!' Georgia said. 'That probably just means they can't prove it. Why would that other woman say she did if she didn't? Women who go in for athletics and sport have to be ruthless—I mean, they train all hours and push themselves through the most ghastly tortures just to win medals.'

'Don't forget the fame, and if they're lucky I believe there can be quite a lot of money,' Penny said cynically. 'If I were you I wouldn't go round talking about it, because sooner or later someone'll tell Jan, and then the fat will be in the fire. That family don't sit down and cry when they're attacked. The newspaper that printed the original story had to retract it and pay Anet large amounts of money.'

'Which she gave to charity.' Georgia's tone revealed exactly what she thought of that.

'Good PR,' Penny said cheerfully. 'You know that—it's your job, for heaven's sake!'

The snort that followed had to come from Georgia, and after that there was silence, presumably while they repaired their faces. Anet looked down at hands so tightly clenched that the knuckles were white, and tried to relax the rigid muscles in her neck and jaw. She almost jumped when Georgia spoke again.

'Well, I think Anet did it. I can just see her deciding it was for the other woman's own good! Hypocritical hag.'

'I wonder what happened to her,' Penny said thoughtfully. 'Victoria somebody, wasn't she? I vaguely remember seeing an article about her somewhere—stars of yesteryear, that sort of thing. I think it said she went the drug route and was last seen living in a squat in London.'

'It sounds like something in one of the tabloids. And, like all good stories, it has a moral,' Georgia intoned maliciously. 'Which is, don't get on the wrong side of Anet Carruthers!'

When the door finally closed behind the two of them Anet took what felt like her first breath since she had heard Georgia's entrance. It was horrible to be on the receiving end of such malice.

Had there been a tiny speck of truth in Georgia's assertion that she'd been domineering because Georgia was everything she was not? Surely she wasn't so petty, so lacking in self-confidence? Probably, she admitted, she should have been more tactful about the sunscreen.

It made her feel slightly sick even to speculate about it. Shakily she washed her hands and ran a comb through her hair. Perhaps this was nothing to do with her, merely another incident in what appeared to be an all-out war between Jan and the younger woman.

Georgia's remarks had reinforced her conviction that, given the choice between a boring truth and a spicy falsehood, most people preferred the spice.

'I've ordered coffee,' Lucas said when she returned, 'and then we'll go home. You look as though you could do with a good night's sleep.'

How true.

Anet drank the coffee without tasting it. Then, strung up and wary, she went with him out into the velvet darkness, its soft air perfumed with coconut and fertility, the sweetly erotic scents of tropical flowers like a seductive promise. On Fala'isi it was too easy to forget about willpower and indulge in a voluptuous surrender to sensuous enchantment.

Not the right place, she thought grimly, to be fighting the fierce infatuation that threatened her peace of mind.

Snow and howling winds would be a much better ambience, or the eternal chilly rain of an Auckland spring.

Which was where she would have been, safe from Lucas, if Serena's mother hadn't been taken ill.

An odd pang ricocheted through her. Shattered, she realised that, although she knew she was going to be wretched when this interlude was over, it would be worth it.

Thoughts and emotions in turmoil, she stepped off the footpath and straight into the path of a minibus.

The screech of brakes and a shout from behind alerted her. Her instinctive jump out of the way was aided by Lucas's iron-fingered hand on her forearm. Automatically she flung out her free arm and caught him around the neck as he crushed her against the tensile power of his body. Through the drumming in her ears she heard him swear—short, crisp curses that set off alarms all through her.

Horrified, she pulled back, but his savage grip kept her imprisoned. A faint, distinctive scent of maleness, clean and salty with undertones of musk, set every nerve in her body jangling.

'I—thank you,' she muttered, trying to free herself.

His arms tightened. 'What the hell did you think you were doing?' he asked with a biting intensity that sent shudders up her spine.

'I just didn't see him,' she said hollowly. It was humiliating to be held so effortlessly; her strength was the one thing that gave her an edge, and it was useless against this man.

She could feel it seeping away, replaced by a slumbrous response that dissolved her bones, sent heated streams of fire through her. Like lava, she thought mindlessly, hot and slow and dangerous, utterly relentless . . .

'I'm all right,' she said, trying to sound composed and casual. 'You can let me go now, Lucas.'

But when he released her she was bereft, almost shivering in the warm, humid air, her heart thundering beneath her breastbone, her mouth dry, as though she had glimpsed some unattainable paradise.

'You could have been killed,' he said curtly, and took her arm, marching her across the now empty road.

'He seemed to come out of nowhere.' Even to her own ears her voice was ragged. 'Mind you, I must have horrified him. Most drivers tend to take one look and veer off. I suppose you notice that too; you're big enough to severely damage anything smaller than a ten-ton truck.'

'You seem to have a thing about your size,' he observed, still with that intimidating brusqueness.

Had he noticed her mindless response to him? Too loudly she said, 'I'm a realist, that's all.' Although she moved her arm experimentally he didn't take the tiny hint and let her go. Instead it seemed as though the pressure from his fingers increased. 'I'm considerably larger than most women, and not a few men.'

It could have been the touch of acid in her tone that caught his attention. 'And some men with fragile egos,' he guessed, 'give you a hard time about it.'

'None worth bothering about.'

'I should think not.' They had reached the car. He unlocked the door and held it open. 'In you get.'

He closed the door as she clipped the seat belt up. Through her lashes she watched him walk around the front of the car. He was truly impressive, like some ancient hero, a warrior.

And she was an idiot. All right, so his uncompromising brand of forcefulness roused a whole range of wild and consuming needs she hadn't known she possessed. She'd have to learn to deal with it, because falling in love with Lucas would mean heading down the royal road to pain.

And he would, she thought briskly, practically, be horrified if he knew how he affected her. Although it

was hard to imagine Lucas embarrassed, he'd pity her
if he knew she was harbouring such hopeless emotions.

So she had better not let him see them.

During the short trip home she chatted firmly and
cheerfully about nothing. Her mother and Jan, she
thought ironically as she got out of the car, would be
proud of her.

Scott had left a message. Serena's mother had shown
a slight improvement but it looked as though it was going
to be a long haul. He hoped Lucas didn't have important things to do elsewhere.

'But you do,' Anet stated, wiping the tape.

'Nothing is more important than friends.' His sea-blue
gaze was cool and unreadable, as noncommittal as his
tone. 'So you're stuck with me.'

Getting ready for bed, she thought wearily that for
Scott and Serena's sake she should be pleased that Lucas
had happened to be there when the emergency occurred.

In fact, she thought crossly, as she opened a drawer
in her dressing table, it had worked out very well for
Scott. Perhaps he had a guardian angel looking after
him. The idea brought a sudden spurt of silent laughter,
which faded when she realised that she was staring stupidly at the suede bag in which the miniature nestled.
Carefully she unwrapped it and looked at the smiling
face, so unlike her own strongly marked countenance.

'I'll bet,' she murmured, 'that you didn't have any
problems with love. I'll bet every man who came your
way ended up twisted around one slender, graceful finger.
Just like Jan.'

Jan was tiny, with features as delicate and beautiful
as the woman in the miniature. Dear Jan; they must look
like a St Bernard and a slender Siamese cat together, yet
Jan had always been proud of her younger sister.

'You and Jan,' Anet told the painted woman, 'would
have had a lot in common. I wonder who you were...'

The little portrait fitted easily into the palm of her
hand; she sat for some minutes looking at it until, roused

by the toot of a horn not too far away, she put it away
and, obscurely comforted, went to bed.

The next few days were oddly peaceful. To her surprise
she found that she and Lucas worked well together. It
shouldn't have startled her, because he worked well with
everyone. Although he joked with the islanders who
helped on board and off they had accepted his lead-
ership and authority without a quibble. The second night
after Scott had left Lucas met the elders and tribal
council, spending a long time with them and satisfying
them that he was able to do the job.

Not that she'd had any doubt about that. Lucas
Tremaine was a man whose mana, or prestige, was so
obvious it didn't need to be tested.

The time they spent together was a mixture of heaven
and hell. Anet sank further and further into a helpless
attraction, unable to reason or persuade herself out of
it. She kept a tight rein on her responses, hoping that
the small involuntary signs of her attraction were lost
on him.

She seemed to be succeeding. Clearly he didn't see her
as a desirable female, for which she should be thankful.
She'd have hated him to behave with her the way he did
with the women customers, although as the days slid by
like boldly coloured beads on a string she acquitted him
of flirting.

It was not that simple. What had fooled her was the
combination of his masculine magnetism and a charm
so far from calculated that he didn't seem to know he
possessed it. Sometimes she thought he was playing a
game. His command over his face and enigmatic eyes
kept his thoughts and reactions hidden, and although
he treated the tourists with superb manners it was difficult to read him, to know what was going on under
that compelling and formidable surface.

Yet he had a keen sense of humour and often made
her laugh, and even through the intense physical

awareness of unattainable infatuation she enjoyed the astringent intelligence that was never deliberately unkind, although he certainly didn't suffer fools gladly.

'This must be hard for you,' she'd said quietly once, after he had dealt politely but inexorably with a woman who had been uncomfortably overt in her recognition of his male appeal.

'I'm as capable of controlling my temper as the next person,' he said coolly.

More so than most.

Drifting through days that were sun-heated and drowsy and brilliantly coloured, and nights of blue and black and gold, redolent with the scents of passion and desire, Anet knew she was falling deeper and deeper into a pit that had no exit except through pain and grief and regret.

One evening when they were ready to go home he said, 'You drive, will you?'

Surprised, she got behind the wheel and waited for him to fasten his seat belt.

He pulled it in front of him but said, 'You'll have to do it up, I'm afraid. I've hurt my shoulder.'

Frowning, she reached over, carefully keeping the belt well away from his chest. As she clicked it home she asked, 'How?'

'Grabbing that man falling down the companionway. Don't worry, it's just an old injury—nothing desperate. Rest will have it right by the morning.'

However, a couple of injudicious movements made it clear that the injury was paining him. He didn't wince or complain, but his mouth tightened and the muscles along his jaw tensed.

After dinner Anet suggested tentatively, 'I could massage that shoulder for you if you like. It might help.'

Turquoise eyes hooded, he lifted his head from his book. After a moment he said, 'Thank you.'

'I'll do it before you go to bed,' she said offhandedly, suddenly alarmed by what she had suggested. 'That way it might help you to get a decent night's sleep.'

'I'd be grateful.'

He returned to his reading, but Anet, jittery and strung up, went looking for some sort of oil. Discarding the olive oil in the fridge, she explored the bathroom cabinet and found a bottle of coconut oil. Her mouth curved as she remembered what he'd said on the first morning—"I always feel as though I'm encased in coconut ice."

By the time she finished with him, he'd smell like it too.

I remember everything he's ever said to me, she thought suddenly, looking at the frosted window as she recalled each word, the cool, deep tone of his voice, his expression, the way his mouth lifted at the corners when he smiled, the warmth and strength of his body, the scent, almost subliminal, that marked him out from other men....

Shaken, she fled into her bedroom and sat down on the spare bed, trying to read. However, when the words danced in meaningless formations in front of her eyes, she gave up and went looking around the house for a chair and table that would work together.

'Why are you prowling about?' he asked, looking up from his book.

She explained. 'If I could find a table high enough to put a chair against I could massage your shoulder while you were sitting in the chair, but you're too tall and the tables here are too low.'

'The bed?'

'Too soft. It'll have to be the floor. I'll spread blankets out and put an old sheet I've unearthed over them. It looks like Serena's source of rags, but there's enough material to cover the blanket. I won't be slathering you entirely in oil; it'll only be on your back, so the blankets aren't likely to get stained.' Babbling, she thought disgustedly; you're *babbling*! He's going to think you're a total idiot.

'Won't it hurt your knees?'

She said, 'I'll use a pillow.'

When at last he got to his feet and said, 'I'll shower first,' she was more nervous than she had ever been before a competition—more nervous even than at the Olympics.

All she had to do, she reminded herself as she pushed back armchairs, was be impersonal and concentrate. After all, she was a professional and he was a patient. Deep breathing helped a little, and so did spreading the blankets out and covering them with the tattered sheet. Unfortunately there were ceramic tiles on the floor, but if she knelt on the pillow and kept her shoulders and arms relaxed she'd be all right.

Nevertheless, her heart was pounding when he appeared in the doorway of the room wearing nothing but a pair of cotton trousers.

Without a shirt he seemed even larger than he did clothed, and the gleaming golden skin made her fingertips itch. Anet swallowed. As he lowered himself onto the blankets she poured oil into her hands and held it, warming it with the heat of her blood.

Trying to speak steadily, she said, 'Exactly where is the pain?'

'Between my shoulderblades.'

'OK,' she murmured. 'Take five deep breaths.'

His shoulders and back rose and fell as he obeyed. Across one shoulderblade was a scar, long and thin and straight. A knife, she thought, feeling sick.

Endeavouring to sound dispassionate, she asked, 'Is that scar still tender?'

'Not now.'

Carefully she ran her hands over his spine, smoothing the oil into his skin as her sensitive fingers searched for signs of tension. Supple and fine-grained, the hard layer of muscle beneath giving solidity, his skin made her hands tingle.

When they reached a certain spot he stiffened slightly.

'Ah,' she said. 'Keep breathing.'

Tipping some more oil into the palm of her hand, she focused on the sore spot, trying to ignore the masculine power and grace of his body. Damn it, she thought wearily, why did it have to be so difficult to resist him? He wasn't in the least susceptible to her, otherwise he wouldn't be so relaxed. No doubt when he thought of her it was as good old Anet, an honorary man.

Using the weight of her upper body to provide leverage, she began to make slow, circular movements with three fingers on both hands, moving from the bottom of his shoulderblades to the base of his neck.

'Digging for something?' he enquired, his voice only slightly muffled.

Without stopping, she asked, 'Does it hurt?'

'A little.'

'You're pretty tense there.'

'Keep going.' He clipped the words.

'Keep breathing, then.'

'I am breathing,' he said.

People often held their breath when her clever fingers approached the source of pain, but Lucas controlled that instinctive reaction, his breathing settling into a long, slow rhythm that made Anet feel good. So good, in fact, that she kept the slow, flowing movements going longer than was necessary. She liked to be able to help people— it was one of the reasons she had chosen her career— and there was a deep, intense pleasure in giving Lucas this ease, a pleasure almost entirely divorced from the sheer sensuous enjoyment of his skin beneath her hands.

Oh, God, she thought suddenly, I'm falling in love with him! No, I've already fallen . . .

Her hands faltered. He seemed to be dozing lightly, for which small mercy she was inordinately grateful.

'Finished?' he asked slowly.

'Yes, I think so,' she said. She sounded quite ordinary, even matter-of-fact.

'Could you do my neck? It feels a little tense there.'

'Yes, of course.' She moved her thumbs to the notches just below the lower ridge of his skull. 'I'll have to—' She slid her fingers along the length of his jaw and applied pressure in steady, pulsing movements. 'Yes, that's it,' she said inanely.

The hard sweep of bone beneath the beard-roughened skin sent a shamefully erotic pleasure sizzling through her. He was, she thought grimly, a magnificent creature, splendidly made, so confident in his masculinity that he made her feel weak and pale, as insubstantial as a shadow.

'There,' she said, hoping her voice was hearty and professional, 'that should do it.'

Before she had a chance to get up he stretched, the muscles beneath that golden skin moving fluidly and freely so that her stomach clenched and the bones at the base of her spine were assailed by a delicious, forbidden liquidity. She only just had time to regain control of her expression. Almost immediately he turned and looked up at her, his eyes narrowed and heavy-lidded.

'You have amazing hands,' he said, his voice husky, and reached for her.

Anet found herself held—without threat but purposefully—against his wide, warm chest, her mouth poised a few inches above his. Dazzled, every sense at once alert and languorous, she fell into the splintering blue-green depths of his gaze.

It was capture, pure and simple, and without resistance she yielded.

'Anet,' he said thickly, and pulled her the last inch so that their mouths met.

Anet had made love with Mark, the man she had once been engaged to, several times; he had kissed her often. She had enjoyed the kisses and the lovemaking, yet when Lucas's mouth took possession of hers she knew she'd never been kissed before, never experienced anything like the incandescent response to his touch that flamed through her every cell.

Although his mouth was warm and demanding and hungry he didn't deepen the kiss, apparently understanding that her passivity indicated surprise, not invitation. However, surrender was not far behind. Almost immediately her muscles became lax, flowing like warm honey until she collapsed onto him as he took his pleasure of her mouth. He was hard and hot, the most wonderful mattress in the world.

Eventually he cupped her face in his hands. 'You kiss like a houri, with a voluptuous innocence that is addictive,' he said in a raw voice, his eyes fierce, and piercing as shards of aquamarine.

Anet swallowed, unable to assemble her scattered thoughts. Compelled too late by a sense of self-preservation, she tried to pull away.

So swiftly that she didn't have a chance, his hands left her face and slid across her back, keeping her against him, breast to chest, the thunder of his heart pumping against her soft bosom. 'It's too late for that,' he said, and in his eyes, his voice, there was a warning.

That long kiss should have blurred and gentled the outline of his lips, but although they were fuller there was no lessening of the determination that marked his face. She didn't need to feel the pressure against her thigh to know that he wanted her; it was there in his face, in the unsparing depths of his eyes, in the faint, feral scent of aroused male.

She should leap to her feet and get the hell out of there, fast enough to scorch a track into the floor, but she couldn't move, couldn't summon the energy to do anything.

He wanted her; she could hear the words echoing through the furthest reaches of her brain. It was like being given hidden treasure, made ruler of the world. When he kissed her throat she was consumed by a sharp, almost painful ache, unlike anything she had felt before.

It robbed her of willpower. Slowly, as though he was inhaling her essence, his lips caressed the smooth length of her throat. The moment they reached hers she opened her mouth and drowned in heated, consuming sensuality.

The kiss he had given her before had been gentle, almost tender, but this was not. This was intense and primal, and instead of being afraid she responded with a matching need.

His white-hot hunger burned through her defences, leaving her exposed and quivering beneath the turbulent demand of his mouth. For the first time in her life she understood what desire was, that passion could ricochet like fiery bullets, blasting its way through the beliefs and restraints of a lifetime.

For whatever the reason, here and at this moment Lucas Tremaine wanted to take Anet Carruthers to bed, wanted to make love to her with all of the strength of his big, lean body. And oh, how she wanted him, almost enough to forget that for men sex didn't necessarily involve love or even liking. More than anything she craved this blazing carnality, wanted to give in to the erotic sensations scorching through her body.

'You have eyes like moonstones,' he said at last against her mouth. 'They were almost the first things I noticed about you.'

Dazed, Anet lifted her head. Something smouldered in his gaze, darkly elemental, almost frightening.

'Have I?' she said, through lips that were tender and stinging.

He laughed deep in his throat. 'Cool and shimmering and translucent, so that it's impossible to see below the surface. I knew the passion was there,' he said. 'That relentless control is a dead give-away.'

He kissed her eyelids closed, smoothed back the vulnerable wings of hair at her temples with tender hands, and bit with gently savage satisfaction the soft lobes of her ears. At each tiny caress her heart sped up and those feverish onslaughts of sensation hurtled through her again, gathering and intensifying in the pit of her stomach before rebounding again, charging her every cell with a wild electricity. An ache throbbed into existence between her legs, where she pressed against his aroused body. The relentless heat of passion built and built, and the smell of coconut oil clung to her nostrils, cloying, almost suffocating her.

Until he said in a voice different from any she had ever heard him use before, 'Anet, I don't think this is a good idea after all.'

His arms were still around her, his body taut with need, but some instinct warned her of his withdrawal. The enchantment cracked and shattered and splintered into shards, exposing her heart to the cutting, icy wind of common sense.

Rigid with disgust at the memory of her behaviour—like a bitch on heat, she thought—she realised that she had to somehow salvage some pride and get out of there before she disintegrated in front of him.

Drawing an agonising breath, she mustered every scrap of strength and will and pulled away. 'You're quite correct; it's not a good idea,' she said, awkwardly getting to her feet.

His narrowed eyes scanned her averted face. 'Anet—'

'It's all right,' she interrupted, refusing to endure any explanations and excuses. Two months before the Olympics in which she'd won gold she'd listened as Mark had explained that he no longer wanted her, that what he had thought to be passion was nothing more than affection; Mark's pity had left her raw with humiliation, and she couldn't take anything like that from Lucas. 'Massage is a very sensuous experience—men quite often get aroused. Don't worry about it.'

His eyes narrowed. 'I see,' he said after a moment.

She sent a swift, meaningless smile in his direction. 'It happens all the time.'

He waited until she was almost out of the door before asking silkily, 'And do you get aroused all the time? Is that quite normal too, Anet?'

The merciless questions stopped her in her tracks. She had her back to him; she didn't dare turn because she was afraid of what she might see in those autocratic, disciplined features.

'No,' she managed, 'but it can happen if the patient is attractive enough.'

Once inside the sanctuary of her bedroom she walked across to the window, staring out at the clump of banana palms with their huge leaves like tattered flags in the brilliant tropical moonlight. Someone had draped one of the hands of fruit with dark, opaque plastic so that it looked like a massive rubbish bag, a brutally prosaic note in the glory of silver and black that was the soft night. A bird called, slow and soft and sweet, the gentle notes rippling in a dying fall.

As though drawn by the soft witchery of sound, Lucas walked out onto the deck and stood outlined by the light of the streetlamps. Anet didn't move. In the distance the rollers purred against the reef, ending a journey of thousands of miles across the wide, warm Pacific—home of storms, birthplace of paradise. A breeze suddenly rustled past the stiff fronds of the coconut palms and Lucas swung around and went back into the sitting room.

God, Anet thought, shivering. Oh, God!

It took all of her self-control to make herself go out to breakfast the following morning. Lucas was up before her. As she came into the room he set an omelette onto a plate, then turned to put it in her place at the table.

She had dressed carefully, even putting on make-up instead of waiting until just before she left the house as she usually did. She needed armour.

'Eat up,' Lucas said without expression.

She sat down and picked up a knife and fork.

'We need to talk and there isn't time,' he said calmly. 'That's always the problem with the morning after the night before. And I refuse to discuss anything when I know I'm going to have to break off halfway.'

'There's nothing to discuss.'

'Of course there is. But if you don't get that eaten in five minutes I'll go ahead and you'll have to get a taxi.'

Baulked and furious, she ate the omelette. It was, of course, excellent, but as they'd been taking turns to produce the meals she had known it would be.

The rest of the day passed in an atmosphere of stiff professionalism. Dreading the evening, Anet was troubled by a sense of rapidly approaching doom that coalesced mid-afternoon into a headache.

She kept silent during the drive home, closing her eyes against the savagery of the sun as it sweltered towards the horizon. Unfortunately blanking out one of her senses increased the acuteness of the others; the faint, potent scent that belonged only to the silent man beside her abraded nerves already stretched and tense.

Back at the house she played the messages on the answerphone, listening to the mostly business calls carefully. Among them was one from Scott.

'All's well,' he announced jubilantly. 'The doctor says she's going to be all right! I'll be back on the four-thirty plane tomorrow.'

A compound of utter relief and exquisite pain rendered Anet immobile. She stood for a long moment, staring at the wall, then dragged in a deep breath and wiped the messages. As the tape was whirring the telephone rang. Starting, a hand pressed to her thudding heart, she picked up the receiver.

'Annie?' her sister Jan's voice said urgently.

'Yes.'

'I'm at the airport. Can you come and pick me up?'

'Yes, of course, but why—?'

'I had to come,' Jan said tensely. 'I'll see you in a few minutes, OK?' She hung up.

From behind her, Lucas asked, 'Who was that?'

When she told him he said, 'I'll take you there.'

At the airport she went ahead while he parked the car. Jan stood in the main concourse, red hair gleaming, a small bag in her hand, her beautiful face intent and worried as she scanned the crowd. It lit up briefly when she saw Anet, but almost immediately they had disengaged from a hug Jan asked, 'Are you alone?'

'No. Jan, what on earth—?'

Her sister's eyes shifted, refocused. 'Oh—here he comes,' she said, *sotto voce*.

Anet's heart iced over. She didn't like the look on Jan's face, absorbed, intent—even, in a strange way, apprehensive.

Her sister was stunningly beautiful, and intelligent and nice.

That had never been a threat before.

'This is—' she began, but was interrupted by Jan.

'We've met,' she said, smiling with a serene composure that would have fooled most people. 'At Olivia and Drake's place, just before Lucas came up.'

'Oh. Yes, of course. I remember.' Anet felt as though someone had walked off with the script.

'I did hand on the message about the vitamin pills,' Lucas reminded her, a note of amusement in his voice.

For a moment time solidified; the bustling little airport with its meeters and greeters handing out the leis of highly perfumed frangipani the island was noted for, the porters, the laughter and excitement and embraces—all seemed to come to a halt as Jan and Lucas exchanged glances. In spite of his amusement there was little warmth in Lucas's smile, and his eyes were watchful and unwavering.

And then he stooped to pick up Jan's case. 'I'll put this in the car.'

'Actually, I'd planned to carry Anet off to the hotel with me,' Jan said swiftly. 'I've booked into the—'

Lucas said, 'Oh, there's another bed in her room at Scott's.' And without waiting for an answer he strode away.

'I'd rather go to the hotel,' Jan snapped.

Anet said tentatively, 'Scott's is more convenient for me than a hotel, but if you don't want to stay—'

'No, no, it's all right.' Clearly something was bothering her, and clearly she wasn't going to tell Anet until she had privacy. 'Is he living with you?' she asked.

Colour rose to Anet's cheeks. 'Living in the same house,' she corrected. 'What's got into you?'

'Has he asked you anything about the—the business at the Olympics?'

If her sister had swiped her across the face with a wet fish Anet couldn't have been more astonished. 'He mentioned it,' she said in a stifled voice.

'Don't talk to him about it,' Jan breathed as they came up to the car. Beside it, in the shadow of the huge poinciana tree, waited Lucas.

All the way home Jan was at her social best, chattering cheerfully, cleverly, her smile and short bursts of laughter much in evidence. Lucas responded with an urbane wit that was oddly forbidding.

They kept it up for the rest of what should have been a pleasant evening, but Anet couldn't restrain a silent sigh of relief when Jan finally said charmingly, 'I'll say goodnight if you don't mind, Lucas, I really need to unpack. Annie, come and help me, will you?'

Once in their shared bedroom Anet lowered herself into the saggy old cane chair and said, 'Tell me what this is all about.'

Ignoring her suitcase, Jan collapsed with boneless grace onto the bed. 'I ran across Georgia Sanderson at a party last night,' she said tensely.

Anet pulled a face. 'And?'

'She said several things that worried me—little hints spiced with malice. She didn't come straight out with anything—that's not her way. Still, she did let slip that Lucas Tremaine has signed a lucrative contract with one of the big British publishers for a book in which the real story of Victoria Sutter's kidnapping will be told.'

CHAPTER SEVEN

ANET looked down at her hands. Rendered a faint gold by the tropical sun, the nails short and free from varnish, they tightened into serviceable fists.

'Nobody knows anything about that,' she said in a hoarse voice, 'except Victoria. And she won't say anything.'

Almost nervously, Jan said, 'Apparently she has. I suppose he paid her.'

It couldn't be true. Anet refused to accept it. 'And how does Georgia know all this?' she asked sarcastically.

'She does the publicity for the New Zealand branch of the publishers.'

No. For a moment Anet thought that the word had been torn from her reluctant throat, but there were no echoes of raw pain in the air, nothing but the soft scraping of the wind through palm fronds outside.

Her face settled into the expression she had worn after Victoria Sutter had accused her of kidnapping her—the stony mask she'd assumed during the weeks when every photographer in the world seemed to have taken up permanent residence three feet away from her.

'I see.' She folded her lips tightly to hold back a howl of pure, primeval agony.

'What do you think of him?'

It was easy to see the way Jan's mind was heading. Anet said discordantly, 'He's very charming.'

She didn't have to say any more. 'Oh, love.' Jan's voice was softly sympathetic.

'Stupid, aren't I?' Anet said with a painful smile.

'No. I don't suppose a woman exists who hasn't fallen at least once for a total swine. And he's gorgeous—you

126

weren't to know that he's also a bastard. Oh, I could
kill him—'

'This is all speculation,' Anet interrupted on a note
of desperation.

Jan looked pityingly at her, but nodded. 'Of course
it is,' she said. 'The thing is—why else would he be—?
No, that sounds awful, and not what I mean—'

But she was right. Why else would a man like Lucas
show interest in a woman like Anet? Certainly not for
her body, she thought, fighting back nausea—he'd found
it easy enough to call a halt last night.

And not for her mind either. There were plenty of
more intelligent women around, women who were witty
and fun and sophisticated, who could flirt and charm
and dazzle, and who knew how to behave in any
circumstances.

She tried to swallow, was prevented by a mouth and
throat so arid she wondered if she'd ever be able to drink
enough water to moisten them again.

'I'm thirsty,' she said, precipitately heading for the
door.

'So am I. Could you get me some lime juice?' Jan
yawned as she got to her feet. 'I'd better unpack a few
things, I suppose. Tomorrow we'll go to the hotel.'

Anet had just opened the fridge when Lucas asked
harshly from the doorway into the sitting room, 'What
made you feel obliged to call in reinforcements?'

She turned clumsily, knocking the bottle of lime juice.
'I didn't,' she said, like a child accused of some minor
crime.

'Then what brought Jan up here?' Light from the
central fitting highlighted his handsome face, its tough,
autocratic bone structure, the glittering line of colour
beneath his lashes.

Anet shut the door with a bang. 'She came up to see
me,' she said with curt distinctness.

'Really?' The contempt in the syllables cut like a whip.

'Why don't you ask me instead of harassing Annie?' Jan demanded from the doorway, hostility bristling through every word.

'All right,' he said, still looking at Anet. 'What are you doing here?'

'I wanted to warn Annie that you are writing a book about Victoria Sutter.'

There was a moment's silence, during which Lucas transferred his gaze to Jan's lovely face before saying levelly, 'I see.'

'Well?' Jan insisted.

He said calmly, 'I'm not going to discuss it with you.'

So it was true. Anet felt the blow hit her heart.

'No, I don't suppose you are,' Jan sneered.

He had never seemed more formidable than when he said, 'This is none of your business.'

Jan drew herself up. 'What the hell do you mean by that? In our family we stick together.'

'It is,' he said implacably, 'Anet's business and mine. No one else's.' His gaze switched to Anet. 'Did you ask Jan up here?'

'I—no,' she said uncomfortably.

Jan said, 'Annie knows she doesn't have to ask.'

'For you to intrude in her life? Obviously. Tell me, when she was sweeping the opposition before her in field events did you tell her how to train?'

Jan's head lifted with unconscious hauteur. 'Of course I didn't.'

'Then why,' he asked, each word coldly judicial, 'do you feel you have any right to interfere in her life now?'

This had gone on too long. 'Stop right now,' Anet interrupted with a stubborn steadiness that belied her inner turmoil. 'If it's good enough for Jan to keep out of my life, then it's good enough for you too. Come on, Jan, let's go to bed.'

'Anet,' he said, his gaze watchful and measuring, 'why don't you ask me yourself?'

She had to breathe deeply to control the nausea that grabbed her. Stonily she said, 'I don't have to, do I?'

His mouth hardened. 'Apparently not.' He stood back with chilling, automatic courtesy to let her blunder past.

Back in the bedroom Jan gave her a swift look before asking gently, 'What will you do?'

'Scott's coming back tomorrow, so Lucas will soon be on his way to Hawaii.'

'Oh, Annie! I could kill him! Don't look like that—I know this sounds awful, but in the long run it will be all for the best.'

Of course it would. At least he hadn't got more than a few kisses from her. Had he hoped that she'd be easily lured into talking about it, like a goldfish taught to come tame to the hand that held bread? While she'd been made helpless by the dark glory of his lovemaking he'd wanted nothing from her but information about an old scandal.

She should, she thought wearily as she got into bed and turned over onto her side, have known better.

She didn't think she'd slept, but when she woke she realised with night-attuned eyes that the other bed was rumpled and empty. She strained forward, listening.

Jan's voice rose suddenly. 'No!' she said. 'How dare you!'

A bewildering complex of emotions surged through Anet. Into her mind flashed an image of her tiny, beautiful sister held in Lucas's arms, panicking, fighting, but as soon as it had come she knew that it was false. Whatever had caused that note of fear and indignation, it hadn't been a crude sexual approach.

She got out of bed, pulled on her dressing gown and walked into the sitting room. Sure enough, the two figures, one dainty in a floating silk wrap, the other cloaked in darkness and intensely intimidating, stood on opposite sides of the room, and so intent were they on their confrontation that neither saw her.

'Then tell me,' Lucas said, the pleasantness of his tone contradicted by the forbidding immobility of his stance, 'exactly why you are so protective. Or, better still, try to understand, if you can, just what your protectiveness has done to her.'

Jan said shakily, 'I don't know what you mean.'

'I'm beginning to believe you.' He startled Anet by saying, 'Come here, Anet. I want you to listen to this.'

'Why are you attacking Jan?' she asked tiredly. 'Because she told me what you're doing? It makes no difference, you know. I'm not going to help you with your book. This is none of your business.' She tossed his own words back at him with bitter emphasis.

He stopped her from joining Jan by looping his arm around her shoulders to hold her pinned against his side. One angry glance at the arrogant profile warned her that he'd enjoy subduing her. Refusing to enter into an undignified struggle, she stood upright and resistant beside him.

'Jan made it my business when she came here,' he said conversationally.

Small but indomitable, Jan stared at him. 'What else did you expect?'

'A telephone call would have been logical. Dropping everything and racing up to rescue her seems more than a little extreme, although I did notice your attitude at Drake and Olivia's. Both you and your mother spoke of her as though she were a beloved child, not too bright but very sweet. It made me curious. Tell me, Jan, if you were young and intelligent and you were obsessively protected by your mother and sister right through childhood and beyond, what would that convey to you?' he asked.

As Anet stirred his hand tightened on her waist. 'Let Jan answer,' he ordered.

Jan inhaled sharply, but remained silent.

Lucas said, 'Try to put yourself in her place—'

'You don't understand,' Anet interrupted. 'Leave Jan alone.'

He laughed mirthlessly. 'So now you're protecting her. An interesting reversal. Coming to Fala'isi has done you some good.'

Jan blurted, 'You're wrong. You must be wrong.'

'Think about it.' A note of ruthlessness killed the richness of his voice. 'An intelligent child, remember, who grew up thinking that because everyone in her family protected her so purposefully there had to be something wrong with her.'

'No!' Anet twisted in Lucas's grip, her whole attention focused on the white face of her sister. 'Jan, he's—'

'He's what?' Lucas held her effortlessly. 'Ask her why she came racing up here, Anet.'

'She's already told you why,' she said shortly, her chest lifting as she forced herself to stand still. 'Because she heard from good sources that you are writing a book about Victoria's kidnapping. I'm very glad she did, because *you* weren't going to tell me, were you?'

'I'd have got around to it sooner or later,' he said sardonically.

Jan said, 'Yes, when you'd coaxed the information out of her. She's not in your league, Lucas.'

His voice was cool and deadly. 'You see, Anet, in her innermost heart Jan's convinced that I must only be after a scoop on that incident at the Games, because no man would be attracted to a woman like you—a woman so different from her.'

'You can twist things until you're blue in the face,' Jan snapped, 'but Anet knows that—that—' She broke off, and to Anet's horror tears brimmed in her eyes. 'It isn't true, Anet,' she whispered.

Anet exerted her considerable strength to break free. To her bitter regret Lucas let her go; she had a repertoire of painful and underhand tricks she was vengefully looking forward to trying on him.

'It's all right,' she said, sliding her arm around her sister's slender shoulders, for once the comforter. 'Don't listen to him. He's a past master at manipulating people.' Ignoring Lucas, she guided Jan back to the bedroom.

Neither of them wanted to talk about his outrageous accusations. Shivering, Jan got into bed and said, 'Sleep well.' But of course Anet didn't.

How clever Lucas was. He'd turned the whole thing around, contriving to shift the blame for his own perfidy onto Jan.

At least he hadn't taken what she'd so blatantly offered him the previous night. Anet supposed she should be thankful for that. One day she would be.

He hadn't made love to her because he hadn't really wanted her.

She let the thought take possession of her brain, stoically enduring it because she deserved to suffer for her stupidity. Falling in love with a man like Lucas was the most stupid thing she had ever done.

Some time during the night she must have slipped into sleep, a restless doze terminated with a jolt by the telephone's shrill summons.

Squinting at her watch, she muttered a soft curse and sprang out of bed. Jan was waking slowly, grumpily, her red hair like living silk on the pillow.

'Anet, it's Serena,' Lucas said from outside the door. 'She wants to talk to you.'

Clumsily dragging on her dressing gown, Anet went out into the hall, her face set in stiff lines. He held the receiver out to her.

'Hi, Serena,' she said in her husky early-morning voice.

'Sorry to get you out of bed, but I wanted to talk to you, not leave a message. Look, I'll be coming back in about a fortnight's time with Mum, but I'll have to keep her company for at least another week after that, so Scott'll need you for that time. Is that all right?'

'Yes, of course.'

'Good. I asked Scott what arrangements he'd made with you, but like a man he said he hadn't made any!'

'I can stay here until you can take over—for at least another month. How is your mother?'

Serena's voice softened. 'She's coming along really well. The surgeon said there's no reason why she shouldn't be perfectly all right in a couple of months.'

'That's great! You must be so relieved.'

Serena said earnestly, 'That doesn't really describe it. Annie, I know it sounds awful, but I am just so grateful your clinic burnt down, otherwise we'd have been in real trouble. Hang on.' She turned away from the phone and said something. 'Scott sends his love and says he'll see you this afternoon. Is Lucas there?'

'Yes.'

'Scott wants to talk to him.'

Anet called out his name and went into the bathroom, where she deliberately delayed until he had to leave. Offhandedly she said, 'You go on ahead; I'll get a taxi.'

His eyes narrowed, but he didn't say anything beyond, 'Very well.'

Safe behind the frozen mask of her face Anet went into the silent bedroom. Jan was lying on her back, her gaze fixed onto the ceiling.

'Good morning,' Anet said brightly.

'Is it?' Jan made an effort. 'Are you going to work today?'

'Yes.'

'I'll move myself into my hotel.'

'Good idea.' Stilted words, but they were all she could produce.

'Damn all men!' Jan said violently. 'Will you come and stay there too?'

Anet glossed her lips with salve. 'That sounds like another good idea. Scott and Lucas can have the house to themselves.'

'Yes.' Jan sat up, looping her arms around her knees. 'I'm at the Sheraton. Do you want me to pack for you?'

'Thank you, yes.' She straightened, and picked up her hat. 'I'll see you later, then.'

It was an odd day. Anet managed not to look at Lucas, yet every time she went anywhere near him she could feel the dark force of an anger curbed only by his will. Not that it showed. She caught Sule looking at him once or twice, but his control was so seamless that no one else realised that he was in a foul mood.

And when it was all over and her nerves were wrung dry there was Scott beaming on the wharf, almost crackling with energy and his pleasure at being back again.

They had a noisy, superficially cheerful reunion before Scott drove Anet to the Sheraton. 'You won't be wanting to work on a tourist boat after staying here,' he teased, stopping beneath the huge canopy.

Lucas turned to look at her in the back, the contemptuous blaze of green in his eyes sending prickles of alarm across her skin.

She stared him down. 'That way you and Scott can talk over old times,' she said evenly, horribly conscious that the mask was cracking a little.

Swiftly getting out of the car, she smiled at the doorman, and said, 'I'll see you tomorrow.'

Scott grinned. 'Yep. Be down at the docks on time or I'll sack you.'

Scott was a darling. Saying, 'Don't worry,' she nodded distantly at Lucas, then walked into the air-conditioned luxury of the hotel foyer.

And there, waiting for her in the airy bar to one side, so alike that they could have been sisters, were her mother and Jan.

Anet could have wept. More than anything in the world she wanted to crawl into a dark hole somewhere and shut the world out. Now there would be anxious enquiries and tenderness; she'd be watched and cossetted and cared for.

Not this time, she thought wearily.

'Hello,' she said, kissing her mother's soft perfumed cheek. 'This is a surprise! How's Dad?''

Cynthia said, 'Oh, darling, I talked to him last night and he sends his love, but he's in Peru, of all places, doing some deal or other.' Just when you need him most, her tone indicated.

Anet bit back a sigh, noting the worry and concern in her fine eyes. 'I'm sorry you came all this way.'

Cynthia exchanged glances with Jan. 'I know,' she said after a moment, 'but I thought you might need me.'

What could she say to that? 'It's nice to have you here.'

It wasn't enough, but she was unable to produce words that would satisfy her mother. Anet's anguish was too deep-seated to be soothed by any comfort Cynthia could offer.

There followed two days of comparative tranquillity. Jan stayed another night, then flew back to Auckland. Anet resolutely refused to discuss the situation with her mother, and after a while Cynthia stopped asking.

Anet knew her silence and obduracy hurt her mother, but the wound was too new, too painful. It pierced her soul, and she could only cope with it by skimming the surface of each day as it came.

Then Lucas called. 'Got over your fit of the sulks?' he asked casually.

'No.' She hung up and turned away.

'Who was it?' her mother asked tentatively.

Anet shrugged. 'Nobody important,' she said. 'Coming down for a drink before dinner?'

Cynthia said, 'Yes, all right.'

They were sitting in the comfortable bar talking to Leigh Fanning, a middle-aged man who was dazzled by her mother, when a voice said, 'Good evening, Anet— Mrs Carruthers.'

Worldly, elegant, the raw power of his body concealed but not hidden by his clothes, Lucas smiled at them with irony and a tigerish amusement that sent sheer terror scudding icily up Anet's spine.

Numbly she introduced Leigh, and then, without any of them extending an invitation, Lucas joined them. Anet was furious, and yet beneath that, and the fear and the humiliation, there was a deep, secret pleasure so intense that for the first time in days she felt alive again.

As she sat quietly, turning her glass around in her hand, she watched a master win over both Leigh and her mother.

When at last he stood and looked down at her and said, 'I wondered whether you'd like to have dinner with me, Anet,' her mother had to struggle free of the trance imposed by his charm and intelligence to say hastily, 'Oh, but we're dining with Leigh tonight. I'm sorry.'

He didn't like that, but the only sign was a barely perceptible hardening of his mouth and a swift glitter in his eyes that promised retribution as he looked at Anet. However, he said urbane goodbyes and left them.

'Phew,' Leigh Fanning said, looking from Anet to Cynthia. 'Not a man I'd care to get on the wrong side of!'

That inimical parting glance had left Anet so strung up she had to force herself to concentrate all the following day. When Lucas rang the next evening she knew what she'd been fearing.

'You're running away,' he said, not trying to hide the arrogance in his accusation.

'I'm not stupid,' Anet retorted, calling an unusual flippancy to her aid.

'Coward.'

'Possibly; however, as well as not being stupid I'm not a masochist.'

He said curtly, 'We have to talk.'

'I don't see why.'

'Anet, this has gone on long enough—'

Pain hammered her heart. 'I quite agree. Don't try to contact me again,' she said, and hung up.

Her mother gave her a troubled look, but was silent.

Collapsing into a chair, Anet said, 'I don't think I want to eat out tonight.'

'We'll just get room service,' Cynthia agreed. 'I'm not hungry.'

The next morning Scott said casually, 'Lucas is talking about getting his yacht ready and heading for Fiji.'

Anet sent him a keen glance, but he looked as guileless as usual. 'Surely he wouldn't be so foolish. This is the hurricane season.'

'Yeah.' Scott frowned. 'He knows what he's doing. If anyone could survive a cyclone at sea Lucas would be the one.'

She said urgently, 'No one can survive a hurricane at sea!'

'It's happened. Occasionally. Anyway, just because it's the season doesn't mean a cyclone's going to come along. We can go for years without having one.'

'And they can blow up out of nowhere!'

Her agitation must have shown in her tone and her expression, but Scott advised easily, 'Don't worry about Lucas; he's a big boy now.'

She gripped the railing to hide her shaking hands. It was unbearable to think of Lucas setting off across the empty seas that lay between Fala'isi and Fiji; big and strong and confident though he was, and more experienced than most men, with a mastery of both himself and his surroundings that was impressive, he was still only human. Against the predatory, pitiless force of a cyclone he would have little chance.

'But surely—'

'He knows what he's doing,' Scott said again, with appalling casualness. 'Look, why don't you take tomorrow off? You're looking tired.'

'How can I?'

He grinned. 'Remember the backpacker yesterday? The Yank who's dived all over the world? Hair down to his waist and a moustache?'

Yes, she remembered him. In spite of his appearance he had certainly known what he was doing.

'He's got his certificate,' Scott said, 'so I asked him if he'd do a day with us. He leapt at it, and he's quite happy to do tomorrow. You could go shopping, or on a tour of the island with Aunt Cynthia.'

She needed the constant concentration on work to keep her mind away from Lucas, but Scott was so pleased with himself that she couldn't refuse.

'Thanks,' she said, forcing a smile.

That evening she was walking along the dock when she was approached by a young man who gave her a comprehensive, admiring look—the Polynesians, she had discovered, admired large-boned women—and a note. 'For you,' he said with an engaging smile.

It was short and to the point, and although she had never seen Lucas's writing before she knew it immediately; bold, black and legible, it sprang off the page.

I've just unpacked on my boat and I've somehow ended up with Olivia's miniature. If you want it Hone will show you the way to the berth.

'This way,' the boy said, apparently taking it for granted that she'd go with him.

'Wait a minute,' Anet dithered. How on earth had the miniature ended up in his gear?

'What is it?' Scott asked, appearing behind her.

When she explained he said, 'Oh, right. Listen, can you get a taxi back to the hotel? I have a meeting, so I won't be able to wait for you.'

'Yes, of course,' she said, and she followed the boy.

He led her to the yacht harbour, almost empty now of the transient population of sailors who had made the Pacific their temporary home; sensibly, they had all sailed to New Zealand or Australia. A hollowness in Anet's stomach translated itself into fear. Lucas was a devious swine, but she didn't want him sailing those treacherous seas.

The boy motioned towards a rubber dinghy. 'Where is this boat?' she demanded.

He pointed to a sleek black yacht on a mooring out in the harbour and helped her in.

Anet knew why she got in without demur. It might be the last time she saw Lucas.

As the dinghy bounced across the tiny waves she staved off an unholy combination of anticipation and anger by working out how the miniature had got into Lucas's possession. Jan must have overlooked it when she'd packed Anet's clothes, so when Scott had come back, and Lucas had moved into her bedroom, the miniature had ended up in his gear.

Lucas's yacht was anchored in the passage just inside the reef. The dinghy dipped and curtseyed at the trivial assault of some cross waves, sending up enough spray so that she was slightly damp when they arrived beside the schooner.

'Up you go,' Hone said when they got to the ladder. 'I'll hold us steady.'

'Thank you.' She climbed briskly up the side to stand on the deck and look around. There was no sign of Lucas.

Uneasily she walked towards the cockpit. Waves crashed onto the other side of the reef with great bravura. The sound of an engine caught her ears; swinging around, she stared stupidly at the small boat hurtling away from the side as though the hounds of hell were after it. Almost instantly the motor on the yacht purred into life.

'Hey!' she shouted, starting to run back along the deck. Before she'd taken three steps her arm was caught in a grip that wouldn't be denied.

'He's gone,' she said indignantly.

'Young idiot,' Lucas said. 'Come on, we'll catch him up.' He urged her back towards the wheel in the cockpit. 'Hold the bow towards the gap while I get the anchor up.'

Unthinkingly, she did as she was told.

The anchor chain rattled and the tide and wind caught the hull. Grimly she held the wheel until Lucas came back.

'You know,' he said without expression, taking over, 'perhaps your sister is right. You certainly don't have much sense of self-preservation, do you?'

'What do you mean?'

'You fell into my hands like a ripe peach.'

That was when she realised that instead of following the dinghy back to the wharf, he was keeping the yacht on the same course he'd given her.

'What the hell is all this about?' she demanded, so furious that the words were spat out like bullets.

'We are going to an island about six miles away,' he said calmly. 'I asked the friend who owns it if I could borrow it.'

'Why?'

He turned a mocking face towards her. 'Because we need solitude to talk things over,' he said reasonably. 'And as you're proving remarkably elusive this seemed to be the best way to achieve it.'

'Don't be a fool. Take me back this minute!'

'No. I'm kidnapping you.'

Her fists tightened. 'You're what?' she asked in a dangerously low voice.

His smile was a narrow, knife-edged taunt. 'You heard. I'm stealing us some space and time.'

'Scott will—'

'Scott thought it was an excellent idea,' he told her deliberately. 'I told him what I planned to do last night. He's going to ring your mother and tell her not to worry.'

Had Lucas organised the replacement diving instructor? It seemed extreme, but then so was kidnapping her. Anet thought that her fury might boil over entirely. 'I'll kill him,' she ground out.

'Why? He appears to be the only one in your family who thinks you're capable of doing anything other than

throw spears around a sports field without having your
hand held. Scott agrees that your family are all too
bloody interested—and interfering—in your life. For
God's sake, you're twenty-five! How many other women
of your age would have a sister fly up to rescue you,
hotly followed by their mother?' He sounded absolutely
disgusted.

He was right, damn him.

Lifting her chin, she met his implacable eyes with a
hard glare. 'They came because they know how much
that business with Victoria hurt me.'

'They came because they don't think you can look
after yourself,' he said cruelly. 'They think you're a
halfwit—a lovable, easily influenced halfwit, who'll need
their care and protection and direction until the day she
dies. It's a belief you seem to concur with. Other women
who've been crossed in love pick themselves up and get
on with life. They don't rely on their family to take care
of them.'

'Crossed in love?' she asked stupidly, her blood icing
over.

'The fiancé who dumped you just before the
Olympics,' he said, not attempting to cloak Mark's actions with euphemisms.

She said woodenly, 'You don't know anything about
that.'

'Well, you'll have time and solitude to tell me,' he
said smoothly.

Sheer rage made her flash back, 'I wouldn't tell you
anything if my life depended on it.'

The smile he gave her was lazy and insolent.

'You're an arrogant oaf.' She could barely spit the
words out.

He flung his head back and laughed, and Anet could
have slapped his face with all her considerable strength
if the yacht hadn't been pitched sideways by a comber
breaking through the gap.

Muttering the worst curse she could think of, she grabbed the edge of the chart table.

'Sit down,' he commanded. 'It would be much more pleasant if we put the sails up, but if I did I suppose you'd wait until my back was turned to try and swim back, or something equally desperate.'

The thought had occurred to her, but she knew her limitations. Excellent swimmer though she was, she wouldn't make it back to shore without at the very least getting a severe case of sunburn. 'I despise you,' she said between her teeth.

'I know.' It didn't sound as though he was in the least worried.

She remembered something else. 'Is my miniature here?' she asked fiercely.

'Of course it is.' His eyes were suddenly stern and penetrating. 'I don't lie, Anet.'

'Only by omission.'

'You haven't asked me whether I'm planning to do the book. You just assumed I am.'

'I don't want to discuss it,' she said unevenly.

'Why?'

'Because I'm not going to help you with it so there's nothing to discuss,' she snapped, goaded into irrationality. How was she going to endure this?

Her inchoate dreams of reciprocated love—of affection, of friendliness, even—were shown up for what they were: the fantasies of a lovesick brain. Lucas couldn't feel anything for her or he would never subject her to such torment. She glowered at him, big and vibrant and determined, clearly enjoying himself. If only she could get out of this situation with her pride intact she would never, ever allow herself to be so vulnerable again.

'We'll see,' he said. 'And don't think you can retreat into that other world of yours either—the one where nothing impinges and nothing hurts. Because I'll drag you back every time.'

Although his tone didn't alter, an abrasive undernote hooked her attention. She sent him a quick, startled glance.

'Yes,' he said, 'I saw that look on your face in the newspapers after Victoria Sutter went to the Press with her accusations. I've been there, but withdrawal solves nothing in the long run.'

'You've been there?'

'When Cara and the baby died,' he said tonelessly, 'I had plenty of time to decide that life wasn't worth living without them.'

She bit her lip. Against his tragedy her experience seemed minor, barely worth worrying over.

'Somewhere along the way,' he said, 'I decided that blaming myself wasn't going to help anyone. I decided to face facts and survive. You, however, ran, and you're still running.'

'I am not,' she said, repudiating his words with a ferocity even she found surprising. 'And I can't imagine you ever blaming yourself for anything.'

He lifted her hand and held her forefinger to his face, and before she had a chance to drag it away he used his great strength to drive the fingernail down his cheek. Horrified, she stared at the slow, thin line of blood that seeped from the scratch.

'I'm just a man,' he said, his voice deep and cold and harsh. 'My blood is red like everyone else's. It comes to the surface when the skin is broken, just like everyone else's. I suffer from the same insecurities and pain as every other person on this planet.'

He released her hand and she hauled out a handkerchief and held it out. 'Here,' she said unevenly. 'That was a stupid thing to do.'

'Mop it up yourself.' He didn't even look at her.

And because she couldn't bear to see the blood on his cheek she did, keeping herself as far away as possible.

'It's all right,' he said, a whipcrack of contempt in his voice, 'I have no intention of ravishing you at the moment.'

'I thought—' she said, and stopped, snatching back the scrap of material stained with his blood.

'I know what you thought,' he said curtly. 'It was patently obvious. You really believe I planned to seduce the information I wanted out of you. I don't think I've ever been quite so angry in my life before.' His voice was icy with barely curbed rage.

Anet attacked in turn. 'What else am I to think? Why didn't you tell me what you intended to write about? Why are you raking up old scandals? You can't need the money that badly.'

She had hoped to pierce that armour of self-sufficiency, but he merely smiled. 'I don't need the money at all. Don't you think that people deserve to know the truth?'

'For important things, yes. But this is athletics, for heaven's sake. Boiled down to the basics, athletes entertain people.'

His brows lifted. 'Is that how you saw yourself? As an entertainer?'

Too late, she realised that anything she said could well end up between covers for millions to read.

Shrugging, she walked away from him to the other end of the cockpit and gazed blindly at the blue, bright sea. A flying fish hurled itself from the water in a frenzy to escape the predators that were chasing it and its fellows. That was how she felt. She had only to look along to the wheelhouse to realise that the man who stood there was not going to let her go until he had what he wanted.

It would have been a lot easier if he had merely wanted to seduce her, she thought with a twisted, humourless smile.

When he didn't speak she concluded that her intransigence was probably irritating him.

And, because she suddenly couldn't bear to be within sight of him, she went below. Cleverly fitted out, with no expense spared, the yacht had been organised for a very tall man. Looking around with pain-filled eyes, she realised that it was the only yacht cabin she'd ever not felt stifled in.

Collapsing onto a comfortable built-in seat, she scrutinised the neat galley, with freezer and fridge and a stove on gimbals. A tightly packed row of books ran above the opposite seat; none of his, she noticed. Her eyes fell on two albums of photographs. Compelled by some deep-rooted curiosity, she pulled one of them down, trying to satisfy her conscience by telling herself that he wouldn't have had them there if they'd been private.

She suffered a suitable punishment, for the first photographs were of him with his wife.

CHAPTER EIGHT

CARA TREMAINE had been tall, almost as tall as Anet, but she had been willowy and graceful, and exotically beautiful. Cuddled into Lucas's arm, her happiness blazed so intensely that Anet shut her eyes.

Close the book, she commanded her nerveless fingers. Then put it back. You don't have the right to look at these.

Yet a deep compulsion fixed her gaze onto Lucas's pictured face. It was harder to read, but beneath the compelling beauty of his features she thought she saw something she had never seen in his expression—the aspect of love.

So now you know, she told herself, and forced her shaking fingers to close the book and replace it.

She couldn't stay there, with the poignant memories of his past happiness. Wearily, her bones aching as though she was feverish, she climbed the short companionway into the cockpit, and without saying a word walked to the railing.

Lucas didn't acknowledge her return, but even with her back to him she could feel his presence at some intimate, cellular level, and knew that she was so lost in this tyranny of love that she couldn't escape its consequences.

Blindly she stared over the side, letting her heavy-lidded eyes unfocus, barely noticing a pair of dolphins that leapt from the bow wave, sinuous bodies gleaming in the sunlight, their smiling faces benign as those of old sages. They had probably sent the flying fish fran-

146

tically leaping along the surface of the sea. 'Nature, red in tooth and claw', she thought. Well, tooth anyway.

Not very much later they arrived at an islet, an outlier to Fala'isi's high island. A quirk of the currents had formed a passage through the reef into a small cove edged by blinding white sand. Coconut palms lined a path of crushed stone that wound its way to a sprawling house on the crest of a low rise.

The engine cut off. Lucas pressed a button and the anchor rattled down. Still without saying anything, he went up forward to check that the anchor held, then strode around the yacht doing seamanlike things, moving with the lithe confidence that spelt out how much at home he was on board.

Anet stared blindly at the beach and the serpentine grace of the coconut palms that leaned towards their ally, the sea. She could dive in and swim ashore from here, but the island was too small; he'd find her in no time. The sun was heading towards the invisible barrier to the other half of the world. Soon it would be a little cooler.

'Do you want a drink?' Lucas asked.

She was thirsty, and it would be stupid to suffer just because she despised him.

'Yes, thank you,' she said politely. 'Fruit juice would be lovely, if you've got some.'

He brought her watermelon juice, pink and vibrant, enormously refreshing, in a tall glass.

With disciplined patience he waited until she'd finished, then said, 'Anet, you must realise that we have to talk.'

It was this which finally set the fuse to her temper. 'Why?' she demanded. 'Why the hell should I listen to you? You can't tell me anything I don't already know. I don't want to hear your excuses, whatever they are.'

'You'll listen,' he said grittily, 'if I have to chain you to my wrist.'

She shrugged. 'Even if I don't believe a word you say? And I won't. Do you think I'm a fool?'

'No,' he said evenly. 'I think you're someone who's quietly driving me out of my mind. For heaven's sake, stop shutting me out and listen to me!'

'It's physically impossible not to.'

He walked across the cockpit and stopped in front of her. Cool and guarded, his eyes glittered in the hard, autocratic framework of his handsome face.

'All right, then; first things first. I want you,' he said conversationally.

The world froze. Waves crashing onto the reef stopped, their crests held in stasis; a couple of lonely seabirds were pinned to the burning bowl of the sky; the steady surge of the trade winds faded to silence in the rustling fronds of the coconut palms.

He was lying. He had to be lying. And the pain of it almost tore through the fragile shield of her composure.

'Quite desperately, in fact,' he went on. 'And I've been trying to work out how to deal with this situation we find ourselves in.'

'What situation?'

'This one,' he rasped, taking the glass from her hand and putting it down on the seat.

She realised what was coming just in time to get herself ready. Her fist clenched, and as he pulled her into his arms she hit him on the side of the jaw with all the strength she could muster. The pain of the blow brought tears to her eyes; it felt as though she'd broken every bone below her wrist.

Cradling her sore fingers in the other hand, she watched him stagger, her fierce satisfaction only dying when he straightened up and she met his eyes. Feral, for once transparent, so that she saw beneath the density of hue to the raging emotions beneath, they drove everything but flight from her mind.

Ignoring her maltreated hand, she turned to run but he caught her, slinging long arms around her waist and hauling her against him. The fitness and strength she prided herself on were nothing. Without even trying, he held her imprisoned.

A wildness that banished thought roared through Anet in an exhilarating surge of power. Baring her teeth, she fought him with every dirty trick she had ever learned. She got nowhere. Oh, she could feel her blows register, yet he countered her attacks with only as much force as he needed to stop them, so that although she grunted periodically with effort it was never with pain.

Finally, exhausted, she stood dry-mouthed, her eyes glazed, blood drumming in her ears. Sweat ran down her face and collected between her breasts, every over-stretched muscle ached, and there were places where his fingers had bitten deep into her skin, but although she was beaten, and she knew it, she gloried in a savage exultation. The furious struggle had satisfied something deep inside her, venting the violent emotions, the agony of betrayal that had been festering these past days.

'I knew you'd be a wildcat,' he said, sounding almost satisfied.

Deliberately, taking his time, he forced the hand she'd hit him with upwards, exerting his strength so that she felt like a puppet. His eyes gleamed as he pulled it against his mouth; his lips on the knuckles drained her of strength.

'They're going to hurt tomorrow,' he said, and touched the sore skin with his tongue in a caress as erotic as it was unexpected.

Anet's stomach clenched. How could rage be so easily replaced by this primitive, mindless need?

'It was worth it,' she said tightly.

His chest lifted as he laughed deep in his throat. Releasing her hand, he said, 'You look as though you'd like to rip out my jugular.'

'I would,' she said.

He angled his chin so that the long expanse of his throat was exposed to her fist. In the hollow at the base his pulse throbbed heavily. 'Go ahead, then, lady.'

Like him, she was breathing hard, and now the passionate heat in her body was relayed and intensified by his. She said, 'Aren't you afraid I might do it?'

'I've had your hands on me,' he said. 'I'd like to feel your mouth and teeth on me too.'

'That's enough,' she said stiffly. 'Let me go.'

He looked down at her, his eyes blazing, at once cold and hot, turbulent and controlled. 'Is that what you really want?' he asked, with a calm assumption of authority she found intolerable.

'Yes!' she said between her teeth.

He didn't move, but she could see the moment he decided to change tack. 'Why do you find it so difficult to believe that any man could love you?'

'I'm perfectly lovable,' she said curtly.

'But not sexy, or desirable, or able to inspire passion,' he finished shrewdly. 'You simply don't connect those words with yourself, do you? I realised that when we danced together that first night, and you were so startled at the effect you had on me.'

'That was Georgia,' she blurted. 'She was dancing in front of us—' Furious with herself, she bit off the betraying words.

He looked at her for a long time, his eyes oddly opaque.

'What are you thinking?' she demanded, when she couldn't bear that scrutiny any more.

'That you divide men into two sorts,' he said judicially. 'There are those who don't find you particularly physically attractive. You're fine with them—you relax, you joke with them and tease them, it's all very friendly. Then there are the poor sods who do find you attractive, and you categorise them as heartless charmers—because, after all, what man would want to take you to bed? They have to be lying. It's a no-win situation for everyone—everyone but you. You don't have to worry about falling in love—you just cut them off dead and the problem of dealing with your own sexuality goes away.'

Seething, she retorted, 'That's not true.'

'You forget,' he said, 'I've seen you in action. Any man who comes on to you is ignored.'

Dragging her gaze away from the mesmerising intensity of his, she strove desperately for objectivity. He was holding her so close that she could feel the muted thunder of his heartbeats, catch the subtle, arousing scent that would haunt her for the rest of her life. Desperately she tried to remember why she was so angry, why she had to keep her head, but it was all slipping away, engulfed by a driving need she couldn't restrain.

Much more of this and she'd cave in, betrayed by her own hunger. 'You're wasting time—yours and mine,' she said insultingly.

He stayed still for so long that she dared to snatch a look at him. It didn't bring her any comfort. A hard, humourless smile curved his mouth.

'Nevertheless, you'll listen to me,' he said at last, and released his grip on her, leaving her off-balance and still angry, her skin tight and stretched as though she'd been baking in the sun.

He went on, the very quietness of his voice rendering it impossible to shut out the words. 'When I saw you something happened, something I'd never experienced before. It gave me a hell of a jolt and I was afraid of its power and intensity, so for the first week or so I kept telling myself that it was just simple, uncomplicated desire.'

Very crisply, because it hurt unbearably to hear him lie, she said, 'I find that hard to believe.'

'That I wanted to take you to bed?' His smile was ironic. 'You knew I wanted you the night you massaged the kinks out of my spine. Why is it so difficult for you to accept that? Because you're taller than most women, and bigger built? What gave you the idea that I follow the herd when it comes to anything?'

She said stubbornly, 'Men don't think of me like that.'

Perhaps some inner traitor wanted physical reassurance—to be swept off her feet—but he made no attempt to touch her. 'How do you know? They actually tell you this?'

Stung by his sarcasm, she said, 'Men fantasise.' Mark had told her that. He hadn't wanted to but she'd needed to know, and eventually he'd explained.

'Were you fantasising when I kissed you?' he asked sharply. 'When you responded with such ardour that I went up in flames?'

He had doused those flames quickly enough, and without much obvious need for willpower. Anet stayed stubbornly silent.

'We have all night to get answers,' he said, the grimness in his voice unleavened by the mockery. 'And tomorrow, and tomorrow night.'

The last amber rays of the sun picked out the classical contours of his face, exposing an unsparing determination that broke her will. 'No,' she admitted with enormous reluctance.

He said grimly, 'Just as well. I don't like competition, even mental competition. Especially that. I have a pretty good idea why you so earnestly believe that you're not a desirable woman, but—'

Hardly breathing, she said, 'I've just been looking at your photograph album.'

There was a short, tense silence until he said through unmoving lips, 'Go on.'

'Your wife was beautiful.'

Another silence, infused with ominous overtones, before he said, 'She is dead.'

'But you are not.' She kept her gaze on him, because she had to know what he was feeling. If there was the remotest possibility of happiness for them together she'd grab it with both hands. But even she, fathoms deep in love though she was, understood that she couldn't build any sort of life with a man who was still in love with his dead wife.

She scanned the formidable beauty of his face, shaking inside at the ruthless control he imposed over his features. Mixed with the anger in his expression was another emotion that brought the tiny hairs in her skin to full alert.

'What exactly do you mean by that?' he asked.

Her tongue stumbled over her words. 'Athletes—good athletes—are born with the killer instinct. It can't be given to them. Part of that is a total refusal to accept second-best.'

He swore, the soft, silkily vicious syllables filling her with a kind of horror. Finally he said, 'So we're at an impasse. You won't believe that I can want you.'

When she didn't answer he waited a moment before continuing harshly, 'You've let yourself be brainwashed by your parents and your sister. Oh, I'll admit they didn't do it deliberately—'

'They didn't do anything. They're just naturally protective. They love me, damn it.'

'And it's a nice, safe, unthreatening love. You heard me talk to Jan. Didn't you discuss it at all?'

'Why should we discuss your attempts at pop psychology?' She forced scorn and disdain into her tone.

'I can tell you why you shouldn't,' he said, with icy, controlled menace. 'Because if you actually allowed yourself to talk about it you might upset the balance of power in your household. Well, we're going to discuss it right now. And, just so that you can't mistake what

I mean, I think that your mother and father and sister, with a lot of help from that ignorant oaf of a man you were engaged to, have managed to convince you that you've missed out on the ability to attract a man sexually.'

'Why not add Scott to that list?' she said deliberately. 'After all, he's convinced that you aren't going to harm me. If I were any other woman he'd assume that you'd brought me out here to seduce me.'

'Scott knows me. And, unlike your family, Scott has never pitied you.'

'That's a foul thing—'

'Damn it, Anet, *think* for once, instead of taking refuge in indignation!' The superhuman restraint splintered; his voice was harsh with barely leashed frustration. 'I've watched you on television and through binoculars when you were competing, and I've always been intrigued by something about you that I couldn't understand, but by the end of that first day on the boat I realised what it was.

'You had absolutely none of the small gestures or inflections or movements, none of the body language that indicates a woman is interested in the opposite sex. I thought you might be a lesbian, but you didn't show any signs of that either. You appeared completely indifferent.'

'Not everyone falls at your feet or makes their attraction as obvious as Georgia,' she said waspishly. 'It didn't occur to you that I might simply not be interested in *you*?'

His voice hardened. 'I'm not conceited; plenty of women find my size intimidating and off-putting. But you, of all women, wouldn't. You move and walk with complete confidence. It frustrated the hell out of me when I realised that I wasn't getting through to you at all, so I slightly exaggerated a sore shoulder and got you to massage it.'

'You had a damned nerve,' she snarled, knowing why
he was putting her through this and despising him for
it. His book must be of vital importance to him if he
was prepared to lie so blatantly. She knew exactly how
men reacted to her, and it wasn't with the elemental
awareness of man for woman.

His smile was cynical. 'It goes with the job. But
although I cheated a bit about my shoulder, it got the
right results. You went up like dynamite in my arms. I
cursed myself and cursed the bloody book, because all
I wanted to do was take you to bed and burn with you—
lose my mind in your dangerous, incredible fire. But I
couldn't do it. Making love before I told you about the
book would have been foolish and unscrupulous. You
deserved to know about it. So, although it was the
hardest thing I've ever had to do, I called a halt. And
the stupidest thing I've ever done was let you run out
of that room without telling you.'

'Why did you?' she asked sweetly.

'Because I was furious. If you remember you told me
that my arousal meant nothing, that it happened all the
time—that massage was a very sensuous experience! You
sounded like a high school teacher explaining the facts
of life to the fourth form. I thought I'd let us both cool
down and then we could talk the book over. But then
the cavalry galloped up. Jan will never know how close
she came to being thrown out of the house that night.
You retreated back behind the barriers, and, because
your response shocked the hell out of you, you weren't
going to ever let me inside again, were you?'

She snapped, 'You know me so well.'

'Better than you do,' he returned caustically. 'You
don't relate to words like "sexy" or "desirable" or
"beautiful". You treat men with the good-hearted
cheerfulness of a friend, and most of them take you at
your own valuation. When one doesn't, you airily inform

him that it's a purely physical reaction brought on by massage!'

'Like you, I realised that it was time to call a halt.' Colour heated her skin, but she stared belligerently at him.

He said violently, 'We're not getting anywhere, slinging accusations back and forth. I want to get this damned book out of the way first. It's about super-athletes. Although steroid abuse does figure quite largely, it's not written about just that subject. I want to know why you stayed off steroids and Victoria Sutter used them. Oh, yes, she's admitted it. I intended to tell you what I was doing before I interviewed you.'

Humiliation ate into her like acid. 'Damned decent of you,' she said, letting the sarcasm drip through her voice.

He didn't respond to her open, savage provocation. Backlit from behind, by the brilliant, smoky radiance of the sunset, he looked like some lean, unyielding hunter from the dawn of time—tireless, without mercy in the pursuit of his prey. 'Initially I decided not to tell you about it because I knew you'd be defensive, and I wanted to see what sort of person you were, whether I could trust you or not.'

A note of—desperation? frustration?—roughened his voice. 'I pride myself on my logical brain, on my ability to read people. I didn't expect to lose every ounce of common sense the moment I saw you.'

God, she wanted to believe him so much she could feel the wanting in her mouth, drumming through her body. But she said, 'So I'm necessary for your book?'

Night was falling with the swiftness and drama of the tropics. Lucas said in a voice that was hard and unrelenting, 'Yes.'

As she turned away he said urgently, 'I know that the thought of appearing in it is repugnant—'

'*Repugnant?*' She whipped her head around to meet the intense, consuming fire of his gaze. Softly, bitterly, she returned, 'Repugnant isn't even halfway to how I feel about it. Lucas, take me back to Fala'isi.'

'I want you to trust me,' he said. He looked at her with antagonism, his jaw jutting hard against the soft purple-blue of the sky. 'But it's not going to happen, is it?'

'No,' she said calmly.

'All right.' He spoke just as calmly, each chilling word incised in ice. 'I know when I can't win. I'm leaving tomorrow. Get on with your safe, sterile existence, Anet. But sometimes—just occasionally—you might ask yourself whether you could have made something more of your life if you'd had the courage to break out of the limitations your family put on you—limitations you've accepted because you can live very comfortably inside them. Slaves live in chains, Anet.'

He turned and strode back to the wheelhouse. Anet watched him, her whole being aching. She wanted to call him back, to take whatever it was that he offered—not love, oh, she didn't expect love, but she'd be happy with anything he could give her.

But even as she opened her mouth to say his name she knew it wasn't enough. The image of his wife danced behind her eyes; even if his book didn't stand between them, there was no way she could live up to Cara, who'd made Scott feel that to be alive was a wonderful thing.

Back at Fala'isi, Lucas took the boat right into the wharf; she jumped onto the wooden pier and looped the bow rope over a bollard, holding the boat steady as he went below. He reappeared almost immediately. 'You'd better take the miniature,' he said, his voice level and unemotional.

They were the first words he'd said since they'd left the islet.

'Oh, yes, I'd forgotten,' she said stupidly, not moving.

'You're quite safe.' The bite in his words made her shiver in the thick darkness. 'Here.' He tossed it over.

Normally her reactions were sharp. However, even as she reached for it, the package slipped through her fingers and onto the wharf.

'Oh!' she cried, dropping to pick it up.

'I'm sorry. Is it damaged?'

Desperate to get away, she stuffed it into her bag without looking at it. 'It's well padded,' she said curtly.

'If it is, let me know and I'll get it fixed.'

'It doesn't *matter*.' She tossed the fender down onto the deck. 'Safe journey,' she said quietly.

'Wait a moment. I'll go with you.'

Even the docks in Fala'isi weren't unsafe, but she understood why he stayed with her until he'd summoned a taxi. He was intensely protective; that was why he wrote those grim, remorseless books, because there were people who needed his help.

She refused to look back as the cab carried her away.

Auckland in autumn was hot and humid, although nowhere near as hot or sticky as Fala'isi. The clinic wasn't ready yet, so Anet had all the time in the world, she thought mordantly, to indulge to the utmost her newly discovered bent for self-pity.

It didn't help that her mother and Jan treated her with kid gloves, the old affectionate camaraderie only showing in small flashes.

'He wasn't right,' Anet said one day, when she and Jan were alone in the house.

'Who?' Jan flicked her a startled look.

'Lucas Tremaine.' His name made her mouth feel sour. 'He had no right to say what he did.'

Jan sighed. 'I think he was and did,' she said slowly, 'He's too damned perceptive. I've been worrying and worrying about it, and the more I mull it over the more I realise that I have felt sorry for you. But what he didn't know, and what is very lowering for me to say, is that my pity was a cover for envy.'

When Anet's jaw dropped, her sister gave her a lop-sided smile. 'I think it was because you've always had a real father. I can't remember mine at all. When Mother married Stephen I loved him with all my heart, but as soon as you were born I knew he was more your father than mine because you looked just like him! And you were such a determined kid—so clever, so thoughtful, so good at everything—whereas I was a butterfly. Nobody took me seriously. They still don't. You won an Olympic gold medal and now you're a physiotherapist. I'm an image consultant. They don't really compare.'

'Don't be an idiot,' Anet retorted. 'You do an enormous amount of good. Everyone knows how hard you work with high school kids and mental hospital patients and the women from the refuges—'

'Oh, yes, but—it's not the same.' She sat up straight. 'What happened between you and Lucas? Don't answer that if you don't want to.'

The image of Cara—laughing, her beautiful glowing face lifted to the man holding her so tenderly—flashed into Anet's mind. Sometimes she thought she would die of the pain. She hadn't realised that anguish could drain life of its colour and joy, rob food of taste and make you feel utterly and completely alone.

She said aloofly, 'I told him I wouldn't help him with the book so he went away. I've only just lived the notoriety down, and I'm not going through that again.'

'I don't blame you.' Jan tilted her head to one side. 'He's a fascinating man, though.'

'Yes.'

'And in spite of the way he behaved, you're in love with him.'

Anet shrugged. 'I'll get over it.'

Jan got to her feet. 'Annie—Anet—if you want something you go after it, don't you? You wanted to be New Zealand's best javelin-thrower, and you trained and worked and envisaged yourself doing that until you got there. Then that wasn't enough. You wanted to win an Olympic gold medal, so you worked until you got it. If you want the man to love you, do something about it instead of behaving like a die-away Victorian miss.'

'You make it sound simple, but it's not the same.'

Jan fixed a schoolmistressy expression to her face. 'OK—a little homily from your big sister. You already know this, but perhaps you need reminding. Nothing worthwhile in this life is easy. You have to take risks. Think about it. If it means a little humbling, a gentle blow to your self-esteem, won't the result be worth it? I've never regretted things I've done, even when they might have been foolish, because making mistakes is a part of living; my regrets have always been for the things I haven't done. Only cowards give up.'

Stung, Anet demanded, 'How would you like to love a man whose first wife was a paragon of perfection?'

Jan looked at her with sympathy and love. 'Nobody's *that* perfect—not even Lucas Tremaine's dead wife.'

Her words rang in Anet's ears. Later that evening, as she sat in the window of her bedroom looking across the narrow reaches of the harbour to the lights of Auckland's downtown area, she tried to work out what to do.

That damned book, she thought wearily; everything came back to the book. Lucas had seen an opportunity to get to know her and he had taken it, without telling her why. The fact that he didn't understand the horror she felt at the thought of enduring such publicity again was no excuse.

She caught the benign, almost sympathetic eyes of the miniature on her dressing table.

'A lot of help you were,' she said softly. 'You gave me my love, all right; why couldn't you work the same magic on him?'

On arrival in Auckland she'd checked the frame. Although it hadn't been damaged, the jolt had loosened the small clip at the back, and further exploration had revealed a slim slip of paper tucked between it and the edge of the portrait. Holding her breath, she'd unfolded it, using eyebrow tweezers in case she damaged the paper. It was a scrap of verse in handwriting that was minuscule and extremely difficult to read. It had taken Anet some time to make a copy of it.

I found Love as you'll find yours,
and trust it will be true,
This Portrait is a fated charm
To speed your Love to you.

But if you be not Fortune's Fool
Once your Heart's Desire is nigh,
Pass on my likeness as Cupid's Tool
Or your Love will fade and die.

It had seemed bitterly ironic. Carefully, she'd refolded the paper and slipped it back inside the frame.

Olivia flatly refused to take the miniature back, so she was stuck with it for a while, but she intended to pass it on as soon as she could.

'You did your best,' she said now, 'but I suppose you have trouble dealing with modern men. I wonder why you seem to understand what I'm thinking?'

It was stupid, almost eerie, but something in the painted face gave her the impetus to pull the curtains, then strip off her clothes so she could look at her naked body in the long mirror, to try and see it with a man's eyes.

Good skin, white and fine. Wide shoulders. High breasts, not very big but not inconspicuous. Her gaze skimmed her form, noting that although it wasn't femininely tiny she did actually have a waist. And a good flat stomach; swivelling to examine her back view, she decided that for sexiness she could do with more curve in her buttocks. Her legs were long, but although they were much smaller than when she'd competed her thighs and calves were still solid and always would be. She wasn't soft and tender; beneath that fine white skin there were muscles, honed and taut.

Not exactly graceful, she thought, but not ugly either. On the other hand, how did she measure up in the seductiveness stakes? She scanned her breasts with their pink nipples, then the dark triangle of hair at the junction of her thighs. Suddenly feeling stupid and slightly ashamed of herself, she pulled her nightshirt over her head and switched off the light on her way to bed.

She lay for a long time, her brain aching as she went over and over the same ground.

When she woke in the morning it was with the decision made for her. She would find Lucas and tell him that she wanted him. If he still wanted her enough for some sort of relationship he was going to have to remove her from the book. If that was too big a sacrifice for him—well, she didn't have to be told things three times. And at least she would have tried.

She felt as she'd used to before a competition: oddly serene, every muscle and sinew relaxed yet alert with anticipation, her stomach disturbingly hollow.

He was surprisingly easy to find. In fact, to her complete astonishment, he turned up in the newspaper that morning in a feature article that trumpeted his achievements. At the breakfast table Anet read it greedily, checking the name of the journalist when she realised how adulatory it was in tone. No, it was written by a man. And it revealed that he was staying in one of Auckland's premier hotels.

Now that she was presented with the knowledge, she was extremely ambivalent about acting on it. But when she went up to her room to make her bed the woman in the portrait looked at her with that amused, almost teasing smile.

'Is this some of your doing?' Anet asked. 'Or a complete coincidence? I don't think I believe in coincidences, but the alternative is a bit much to swallow too.'

Scoffing at herself, she set her jaw and chose a dress. Like many of her other dresses, it was a shirtwaister. Although she liked the material, she gazed morosely at her reflection, thinking that since meeting Lucas she had spent more time in front of mirrors than she ever had in her life before.

The dress looked ordinary. Boring. Middle-aged and safe. And she, she thought with a shiver that was a compound of excitement and dread, was no longer satisfied to be safe. She was going to discover the charms of living dangerously.

'I need Jan,' she said aloud, peering down at her shoes. Like the dress, they represented everything she no longer wanted; plain, classic pumps, they were low-heeled so that she didn't tower quite so much over everyone. 'She's the image consultant.'

But this was something she wanted to do—no, *had* to do—by herself. Setting her jaw, she told herself that she wasn't putting off the meeting, merely making sure she gave it due importance.

'Mum,' she said at the bottom of the stairs, 'can I borrow a lot of money from you as well as the car?'

'How much money, darling?'

'I don't know,' she said, aware that Cynthia was scrutinising her face. 'I want to buy some clothes.'

Her mother's gaze slipped across to the newspaper, neatly folded. She opened her mouth, then closed it firmly again before saying, 'Yes, of course you can.'

Anet drove over the harbour bridge and across town into Newmarket, a suburb noted for its excellent shops and boutiques.

Two hours later she walked back to the car, exhausted and slightly green with panic. She had spent more money than she had ever done at one hit in her life, and all of it on clothes such as she had never worn before. Not only had the assistant she'd found been eager to help, she had also procured accessories and told her where to go for elegant underwear, like the satin briefs and bra Anet now wore beneath the flowing trousers and shirt and gilet she had bought.

It had wiped out her bank balance and she'd be in hock to her mother for years, but if it worked it would be worth it, she told herself stoutly.

If it didn't . . .

At least she would know, and the knowledge would drag her out of this limbo she'd existed in since Lucas had left her on Fala'isi.

Still astonished at the difference the clothes made, she glanced sideways at her reflection. 'You're tall enough to carry off these wider trousers superbly,' the shop assistant had said. 'And that grey does wonders for your eyes.'

It did too, intensifying their colour so that they no longer looked transparent and empty. Even her shoes, an elegant suede pair in exactly the same grey as her clothes, looked smart, although she was finding it a little difficult to walk in heels higher than any she had ever worn before.

Just like Cinderella off to the ball in her borrowed finery, she thought, and wondered for the thousandth time whether she had the guts to go through with this.

She dumped the boxes and bags into the boot of the car, got in, and headed in the direction of the inner city, worrying her top lip with her teeth as she manoeuvred through the traffic.

What if Lucas no longer wanted her?

Then he was fickle and not worth bothering about, and in the end she'd be better off knowing, she told the cowardly part of her brain that urged her to turn the steering wheel towards the harbour bridge and flee for home.

At the hotel Lucas was staying in she surrendered the car keys to the parking attendant, hid in the cloakroom for a while under the pretext of repairing her lipstick, and then, ignoring the bar, which lured her with the promise of a little temporary courage, walked across to the desk and asked if they could contact Lucas Tremaine.

CHAPTER NINE

'WHO shall I say is wanting him, madam?' the professionally smiling receptionist asked.

When she gave her name the receptionist's smile turned into something more genuine. 'I thought I recognised you. I watched you win your medal at the Olympics. I almost cried when they gave it to you.'

Sometimes being a sort of celebrity helped. Anet said, 'I did. Very embarrassing, but the tears wouldn't stop coming.'

'Oh, we all knew how you felt. It was a great day for New Zealand as well as for you,' the woman said, punching numbers into a phone. Turning sideways, she murmured into the receiver before smiling up at Anet. 'He wants you to go up, Ms Carruthers. He has a suite on the fourteenth floor—number two.'

Of course he'd have a suite. She remembered him saying once that most rooms were too small for him just as they were for her; it had been a similarity she had cherished.

All the way up in the lift she wondered just what she was going to say, what he would say to her. The fact that he had asked her to come up surely meant that he still wanted her—or did it? Perhaps he just thought she'd given in about his wretched book.

Worse still, perhaps he'd take one look at her in her new clothes and think, Oh, God, she obviously wants me to take up where we left off and I don't want to. He might think she was an utter fool—mutton dressed as lamb—no, no, elephant dressed as mouse...

166

She was staring down at the grey trousers with acute dislike when she realised that the lift had stopped. Hurriedly she looked up and there, framed by the doorway, was Lucas, looking at her with narrowed, enigmatic eyes. He wore a pair of dark trousers and a blue shirt, the sleeves rolled up to reveal his tanned forearms.

Anet's heart performed peculiar gymnastic movements inside her.

'If you don't emerge soon,' he said evenly, 'it will carry you off down again.'

With as much composure as she could summon she walked out, but had to forget dignity and scurry through as the doors began to close on her.

Silently, her brain gone into receivership, she went with him into a large, airy sitting room with a magnificent view over the sea. After a swift glance around the impersonal serenity of the room Anet thought she would probably always remember it, even when she lay dying.

'And to what,' Lucas asked with a coolly unsettling gaze, 'do I owe the honour of this visit?'

If only she could discern what he was feeling, what thoughts were going through that astute brain. But as always he was a mystery to her. One day, she thought dangerously, one day I'm going to be able to look at your poker face and know what you're thinking. It was this conviction that gave her the courage to continue. Taking a deep breath, she said, 'I want to talk to you about your book.'

'I see.' Two meaningless words, but they held a threat and something more.

Anet looked at his guarded face and knew with sickening hopelessness that she couldn't go through with it—didn't have the right to ask him to cut her from his manuscript. Since coming home she had re-read all of his books. He didn't write gossip or sleaze. And, although he tried to distance himself from the subject matter, to be objective and impersonal, his passion for justice and truth reverberated on every page. It was what had made them bestsellers—that and his enormous, angry compassion.

She loved him. He couldn't reciprocate, but that didn't detract from the exhilaration of loving him. And part of love was her desire to see him happy. If she made him produce a book that was less than he wanted, she would be denigrating her own feelings.

Baldly, her steady voice concealing the recklessness beneath, she said, 'I withdraw my objections. I'll help you with it if you still want me to.'

He closed his eyes. Dark lashes, thick against his tanned skin, softened the autocratic challenge of his facial structure. Anet's heart quivered.

Then he opened them, catching her helpless glance, and into the brilliant eyes there sparked an emotion she didn't recognise.

'Why the turn-around?' he asked, his voice level and without intonation.

She flinched. Now, too late, she realised just how much she had banked on his continuing desire for her. There was nothing of hunger in his face or his eyes, merely a keen calculation. But it made no difference. She said, 'I realised I had no right to stop you. I read your books again. It's a cliché, but the world does need people like you.'

'Very altruistic of you.' He paused, then said almost indifferently, 'Well, you don't need to worry any more. I'm not putting you into a book.' The second sentence was delivered with a jarring, sarcastic note.

She thought she hadn't heard him properly. It was what she most wanted, and yet she was seized by a pang of loss, of desolation.

'Why?' she asked.

He shrugged. 'It doesn't matter. Anet, what changed your mind?'

She searched his face, found nothing but cool, watchful self-command.

Well, he'd asked; he could deal with the result. 'I love you,' she snarled.

And had the dubious pleasure of seeing him knocked off balance. His eyes widened, darkened, the pupils expanding to swallow the bright colour, and a muscle flicked beside his mouth. Then he laughed, a low, triumphant laugh that tightened her skin and drained the heat from it.

'Do you, indeed?' he said softly, and pulled her into his arms and held her, his thumbs forcing her chin up so that he could scrutinise her face. 'When did you know?'

'When I was massaging your back.'

His expression went from triumphant to furious. 'Why the hell didn't you at least give me some hope?'

'I was afraid,' she snapped, adding, 'and—disgusted by my behaviour.' The words were heavy with distaste.

Harshly he said, 'I thought you were disgusted by mine!'

'No,' she cried. 'But afterwards—Jan came, and—'

'And you were sure I'd come to Fala'isi to pump you about the book. And you were partly right, although I didn't ever intend to seduce anything from you.'

He touched her cheek, his hand cupping the side of her jaw, lean fingers gentle yet sure. In the depths of his hard eyes a possessive glitter of flame summoned an answering fire from deep within her.

'Listen, and don't ever forget this,' he said roughly. 'I wanted you when I saw you on Scott's boat at Fala'isi—no, even before that. I'd watched you on television and at the Olympics, and I couldn't get you out of my mind. You were like a goddess . . . tall and strong and confident.

'When Olivia mentioned that she hadn't given you your birthday present and that it was too fragile to put in the post, I offered to take it to you. I told myself it was a simple matter of needing your input into my manuscript, and I really believed that until I saw you come out of the water after you'd fished Georgia out. You were gloriously pagan, wild and free, totally confident in yourself, and yet oddly, completely innocent, with no sign of the games other women play. That was when I admitted that I'd come to Fala'isi because I was fascinated by you.'

Her breath gathered in a tight ball in her chest. She couldn't speak, didn't dare answer.

He went on quietly, 'I didn't even want to mention the bloody book. Oh, a couple of times I forced it into the conversation, but it worried you so much I found myself making excuses not to bring it up. I wanted to discover everything about you, to drown in you, to find out how you thought and what you dreamed of, and the damned book barred the way. It was the first time anyone had got in the way of my work. I was obsessed with you, but it made me angry and resentful too, because that hadn't happened to me ever before.'

Anet searched his face. 'Not even with Cara?' she asked diffidently.

'No. Cara was young and loving and afraid, and I would have been a good husband to her for the rest of her life.' His expression was remote, as though he were talking about another man, another universe. 'Her father was the editor of a daily paper. Two weeks after I arrived in San Rafael he was killed by the dictator's henchmen.

'Her brother was fighting with the guerillas in the hills. When her father was murdered she managed to escape and make her way to my hotel, terrified and with good reason. She'd heard the men who beat him to death planning to use her as bait to make her brother surrender. She hadn't been brought up to be tough; her family had protected her and she didn't know what to do.'

'Like me,' she said quietly, aching with sympathy and compassion.

The bleak darkness in his expression lifted as he looked at her. 'Not quite. You're competent, well able to look after yourself. Your family just haven't realised it yet. Cara never had the chance to discover her own strength.'

'And you blame yourself.'

'I was so arrogantly sure I could keep her safe in England, I didn't even take any precautions, much less hide. And I made it easy for those murderers to find us by writing a whole series of articles denouncing the blood-soaked atrocities of the regime. For years I wondered what would have happened if I'd kept sensibly quiet.'

Anet said gently, 'Thousands more would have died, several million been plunged into misery. But Cara and your child might be alive today.'

His smile was twisted, sardonic. 'You don't pull any punches, do you? I'll always blame myself, but at least she didn't know what had happened. She was unconscious when I found her in the ruins of the house; she opened her eyes, but she thought she was back in San Rafael, with her father and her brother. If I hadn't married her and taken her out of the place she'd have still died, but they'd have tortured her first. At least this was quick and painless, and I think she was happy with me.'

Tears scalded the back of Anet's eyes. She sniffed and said, 'She was. You only have to look at the photographs to see that.'

'Darling.' His voice was strained and rough. Taking the two steps necessary to reach her, he pulled her into his arms, holding her with a gentleness she didn't expect. 'Don't cry. Why are you crying?'

She turned her head and kissed his throat, feeling the strong throb of his life force against her mouth. 'It doesn't seem fair,' she said.

Tilting her chin, he looked into her eyes, his own clear and lucent and piercing. 'I don't deserve you,' he said quietly, as though it was a vow, 'but I'm going to try to for the rest of my life, I swear it. Anet, I need you. I've never needed anyone before.'

'Why didn't you tell me this on board the *Dawntreader*?' she whispered.

'I was going to, but I still had hopes of persuading you to talk to me about Victoria Sutter. On the boat I learned how totally opposed you were, and I realised I was going to have to chose between you and the book.' He let her go and walked across the room, his back and shoulders rigid. Crisply, not trying to hide a note of self-derision, he continued, 'It was a choice I didn't want to have to make and I resented it—and you, for forcing me into a corner.'

'So you thought I could damned well stew in my own juice.'

'There was another thing,' he said, as though she hadn't spoken. 'More than I wanted you—and I want you so much that I've been only half alive these last weeks—I needed you to trust me, to accept that when I look at you I see the one woman I need, the only woman who can make me feel like this. But you couldn't believe that I felt anything more than casual lust. You honestly thought you had nothing to offer a man.'

She hesitated, because if she told him this she would be divulging her innermost secrets, and so far he hadn't said anything about loving her.

But he wanted her trust.

Awkwardly she said, 'I—when I was engaged to Mark we made love.'

'I assumed that you did,' he said, taking on the mask of indifference with which he hid his emotions. 'I can't say I like the thought of it, but what happened to you before we met is not my concern.'

As her lashes came down to cover her eyes she ploughed on, 'I need to tell you this, Lucas. I enjoyed it, and I thought Mark enjoyed it too.'

His brows drew together. 'So?'

'But he didn't.'

'How do you know?' he asked slowly.

'I made him tell me. Oh, he didn't want to! He liked me—he was really upset when he came to break it off and he didn't want to hurt me.'

'Yet he told you it was because he found you undesirable?'

Determined to tell him all, she ignored the flood of heat through her skin and said jerkily, 'He said I didn't—I wasn't good—'

'Anet, if you were so lacking in feminine attractions, how do you think he managed to make love to you?'

She bit her lip but said spiritedly, 'I read magazines. Men can—'

Beneath the even surface of his voice she could hear anger and contempt as he interrupted. 'People break off relationships for a whole variety of reasons. People who are dynamite in bed together quite often can't live with each other in any sort of amity. I don't know why your former fiancé, who sounds at the very least to be a thoughtless young cub, broke off the engagement, but I doubt very much that it was anything to do with your sexual appeal or your response in bed. I imagine it was more that he resented your absorption in your sport.'

Mark had hated the long hours of practice and the time she'd spent away from him. She objected, 'But he would have told me...'

'Not necessarily. Not if he was angry with you and wanted to hurt you,' he said with rather chilling detachment. 'It doesn't matter anyway. Anet, your response is all that any sane man could want. When we're married I don't want calm affection or a bloodless acceptance in my wife—I want what you showed me that night on Scott's floor. Total and complete passion.'

'Married?'

She didn't think she had actually been able to articulate the word, but he answered blandly, 'Of course we're getting married.'

'Why?'

He caught her wrist, capturing her by the mere touch of his hand. 'You are going to marry me,' he said, his tone not quite concealing the primeval possessiveness in his words, 'because I love you so desperately that I don't give a damn for anything else, and because I don't want to even consider the prospect of living without you. And because one day you'll feel the same way about me.'

'Lucas?' she whispered, her eyes widening as she absorbed his uncompromising determination. For the first time she began to think that the miniature's promise might be more than a piece of eighteenth-century verse, because in his arrogant features, in the blazing depths of his eyes, she saw unconcealed love—naked, immeasurable.

'I mean it,' he said. 'You don't love me like that yet, but you will one day, my heart.'

'Lucas,' she said, and smiled.

'You have the most beautiful smile.' He pulled her against him, warming her, enfolding her, holding her safely. 'Even when there are tears in those glorious eyes!'

'I always cry when I'm happy. I cried when I got the gold, and I dare say I'll cry when I hold your child for the first time—'

His arms tightened around her, making her gasp. Instantly he eased the pressure. 'Does that mean that you intend to marry me?'

'I didn't know I was being given a choice.'

She could hear laughter in his voice. 'Unfortunately the days are long past when a man could force his recalcitrant woman to marry him,' he said, 'but I have no intention of letting you go. From now on wherever you are is where I'm going to be.'

'That's funny,' she said, smiling. 'That's exactly what I decided last night. Jan told me I was being weak and wimpy, giving up without a struggle, so I lay in bed and told myself that as you were all that I wanted I'd better go and look for you.'

'Am I all that you want?'

How could he not know? It astonished her that he should need reassurance. 'Absolutely everything.'

'Good,' he said with enormous satisfaction, 'because I'm all you're going to get. And that as soon as possible.'

'Of course,' she said thoughtfully, 'there are such minor things as careers and children—'

'One of the advantages of being a writer is that I can do it anywhere, so we'll live wherever suits you. As for children—whenever and however many you want.'

It was too soon to discuss children. Anet wanted to revel in this golden time, these moments of pure happiness. She lifted a glowing face, and he laughed softly in his throat before at last kissing her eager, expectant mouth. Sighing, Anet went under, yielding her heart entirely to him.

Some time later he said against her mouth, 'I have a newspaper interview in a few minutes.'

'I saw the one about you in the morning paper,' she said.

'I hoped you would. That was why I told the journalist to put in that I was at the Regent.' He gave a thin smile as her eyes widened. 'He thought I was boasting. If that hadn't worked I was coming for you, lady.'

No one should ever consider Lucas to be insecure enough to boast. But she might as well give him her complete surrender. Belying soft, smiling eyes with a prim mouth, she said, 'Oh, you didn't have a chance. I went out and bought a whole shopful of clothes to tempt you with—I owe my mother more money than I care to think of.'

He laughed, and touched her mouth, and would have kissed her again if she hadn't held her finger between his lips and hers. 'You'd better brush your hair. I seem to have got it in an awful mess.'

'Stay there,' he commanded as he went to the bedroom.

Dazed with delight, she wandered across the room, coming to a halt by the window. Glowing with the golden mellowness of autumn, the waters of the harbour glittering beyond the elegant Victorian cupolas of the old Customhouse building, Auckland seemed a fairy city.

Smiling, she turned, and saw a fax paper on the floor. She bent to pick it up. A few words caught her eye; she looked away, but their import dragged her gaze back.

When Lucas came back she was standing there with the paper in her hand. 'I didn't mean to read this,' she said, 'but I saw—Lucas, when you said you weren't going to put me in it I didn't realise you were pulling the plug on the entire book!'

His dark brows drew together. He took the paper from her hands, crumpled it and tossed it into the rubbish bin. Lightly he said, 'It's no big deal. I chose you, that's all.'

She said passionately, 'I couldn't live with myself if you did that. The world needs people like you—our marriage will be based on a lie if you stop doing what is important to you just because I can't bear a small bit of notoriety.'

He was watching her carefully. 'It's not quite that easy,' he said slowly. 'I'm compromised anyway. There will be people who'll say that I pulled my punches where you are concerned, just as there were people who refused to believe my articles about San Rafael because I was married to Cara.'

Horrified, she opened her mouth to speak, and he said savagely, 'We're getting married. Forget you ever saw that.'

She pointed to the paper. 'What does it mean, "Now that VS has spilled her guts"?'

He hesitated before saying tonelessly, 'After I'd paid Victoria a considerable amount of money—and presented her with the results of a lot of digging—she told me exactly what had happened before the Olympics.'

Anet sat down. Taking a deep breath, she said carefully, 'Did she tell you that she set up the whole thing because she'd miscalculated her steroid doses, and when the authority wanted to know why she hadn't fronted up for the tests she was supposed to take she came up with some cock-and-bull story about being kidnapped?'

'That's exactly what she told me,' he said. 'She thinks it was a brilliant idea, and that telling you before you competed that she was going to accuse you was another. She still can't understand how you went out and won.' His voice was crisp and angry. 'She admitted it without remorse or embarrassment. All she was interested in was the money. Nowadays her drug of choice is heroin.'

Anet closed her eyes and said, 'Oh, God...'

'Yes,' he said. 'I'd planned to tell you after we married and ask you what you wanted to do with the information. Her admission does remove the small blemish on your reputation.'

She laced her hands together. 'How badly will it affect your reputation if you marry me and don't put this in your book?'

'I'm not going to write the book.'

'Lucas, if you don't write that book our life will be built on cowardice—my cowardice.' A thin sliver of panic stabbed her. His handsome face revealed no flicker of emotion, nothing. Desperately, she continued, 'I can cope with anything if I have you with me. But I couldn't live with myself if you gave up something so important to you. You don't need to make that choice. It isn't fair.'

And then she saw the break, saw the final demolition of the defences he had built so carefully over the years, saw the naked power of his beauty shine forth as he said shakily, 'Anet, my heart's lady, I love you. All right, then; I'll write the book.'

They were married a week later in her local church; Anet had drifted through the intervening days with a smile that wouldn't be banished, while her mother and Jan shook the world by the scruff of the neck so that everything would be ready in time—from the exquisite, classically cut silk brocade dress Anet had chosen, to the flowers. They masterminded a magnificent reception in the house Anet had lived in all her life and they even managed to fit in the acquisition of new clothes for themselves.

It was surprising how many of her friends were able to come. The man who had coached her to her gold medal told Lucas he'd better look after her or he'd hear from him, and Scott and Serena took a couple of days off and flew down from Fala'isi; more relatives than she'd expected turned up, and there was Olivia, and her tall, powerful husband.

'I suppose you're going to say that the miniature did the trick,' Anet said as Olivia, looking sweetly smug, kissed her.

'No, I am not.' Olivia beamed at her. 'I know exactly who did it.'

'Sometimes I wondered whether she actually did organise everything,' Anet confessed.

Olivia exchanged looks with her husband. 'I know the feeling,' she said wryly. 'The lady has a mind of her own.'

Lucas, who had been interested by the tiny poem although dismissive of any supernatural aspects, asked, 'Who was she?'

Drake said, 'We have no idea. It's not signed, but the expert I contacted is sure he knows who the artist was—one of the masters, as you can tell from the work. However, no one seems to be able to identify the subject. We do know he had a long and extremely happy marriage, so my sentimental wife thinks that she was the girl in the miniature.'

'I'm convinced she was. There's just one thing,' Olivia said. 'You have to hand her on.'

'So the poem says,' Anet murmured.

'Did you find a poem? Where?'

Lucas said, 'It's tucked into the back—between the frame and the ivory.' He quoted the lines.

Olivia's eyes widened as she looked at her husband. 'But that's almost the same as the one I dreamed!' she said a little uncertainly. 'I'm not saying I believe it, mind you, but she certainly brought Drake and me together. Don't just hand her on to anyone, though. I know it sounds silly, but I think she tells you when she wants to go.'

She laughed at Anet's expression. 'No, you don't get a veddy, veddy English voice suddenly appearing in your brain saying, "That's her!" but when Lucas rang to tell us he was coming to say goodbye that time, it suddenly occurred to me that you both would look very nice together.'

It was an odd little conversation. With raised brows Anet looked at Drake, who surely was the least superstitious person in the world, but he merely smiled.

'Thank you,' Lucas said, bending over Olivia's hand to kiss it, a manoeuvre he carried out with gallantry and grace. 'I owe you.'

They left the reception for the airport and headed towards Fala'isi, where Lucas had borrowed the islet for their honeymoon. Anet slid into sleep, lifting her head from Lucas's broad shoulder only when the jet began to make its descent.

'We don't have to go out to the islet tonight,' Lucas said as they collected their bags. 'We could stay in a hotel.'

'You'd never get a reservation now.'

His smile was ironic. 'Do you want me to?'

'No.' She had no doubt that if she did he'd organise it, but she needed to be alone with him. They hadn't yet made love, and it seemed somehow right that they wait until they reached the motu.

They went in his yacht; for the hour it took them to get there she stood quietly beside him in the wheelhouse, watching his dark, clever face as he took them through the reef and across the warm sea to the small piece of land, blessedly solitary on its coral reef.

'Would you rather stay on board tonight?' he asked when they were almost there.

She smiled. 'No, let's go ashore.'

There was a moon; not a full harvest moon, but then in the Pacific there was no harvest season. The munificent earth yielded its fruits all year round. This moon was young and unsure, but it soon got the hang of things and spread a wash of silvery light across the water, so that they could see their way into the tiny harbour.

Within ten minutes they were walking up the crushed coral path towards the house.

'Who is this friend who owns the place?' Anet asked as Lucas pushed the doors open.

'It belongs to Grant Chapman, a sort of paramount chief of the island. I know him well, he and his wife. They're in the South of France at the moment and couldn't make it to the wedding, but you'll meet them some time soon.'

He took both suitcases into a big, tiled bedroom dominated by a massive double bed. As he lit a lantern Anet looked around, trying to hide her sudden shyness.

'Anet,' he said, his voice deep and quiet and moved. 'Dearest girl, my own heart, don't look so harried. If you're tired we'll sleep in each other's arms, that's all.'

Although her heart swelled at this further evidence of his tenderness, she sent him a look of pure, undisguised horror. 'Don't you dare,' she said, flushing but determined.

He laughed beneath his breath, those shrewd, sea-blue eyes no longer opaque. What she saw there made her shiver as she realised just how much that mask concealed of the man behind it, how intense were the reactions he hid from an uncaring world.

'Yes,' he said, 'and it's too late for you to run away. I'm not going to let you go now, lady.'

His words, spoken with such stark, elemental hunger, fanned the wildness smouldering deep inside her. 'I'm not going to let you go either,' she said. 'What did you call me?'

'Lady.' He laughed softly. 'I know it's unfashionably romantic, but that's how I think of you. *My* lady.'

'I dreamed about you,' she said, amazed and a little uneasy. 'You were a highwayman. That's what you called me—lady. And you said that I was yours, that you were coming to claim me.'

His smile was wickedly edged, frankly desiring. 'And I was right,' he said. 'I'm sorry it took me a couple of hundred years. Come here and show me how much you want me.'

Want him? Oh, this was more than wanting, this slow, consuming sensation that pulsed through her like the subliminal shock waves from a distant earthquake. This was a craving, a wrenching need, an anguish of passion. She had no tricks, nothing but her love to guide her, so she followed atavistic instincts that had come down to her from generations of women forebears. When she walked towards him he didn't move, his lashes concealing everything but a thin line the vivid, lambent blue-green of the sea under a tropical sun.

She said his name and reached up her hand and touched his cheek, almost crying out because it seared her fingertips.

Colour outlined the harsh, high sweep of his cheekbones. He looked down at her, his mouth tender and fierce, the glittering, glinting light in his eyes piercing her self-possession like a spear, homing into a part of her she hadn't known existed, a part that knew exactly what he wanted, what she wanted, a part that was ready for him on a more primal, fundamental level than that of the merely physical.

He kissed her gently, and then with a white-hot fervour that scorched through the last of her fears, rendering them nameless and without power to hurt. She surrendered her mouth, yielded her heart, gave him power over her apprehension and her inadequacies, and didn't feel any terror because she knew that there was nothing to be afraid of.

One burning, unfettered look from him had chased away the sense of inferiority that had bedevilled her ever since Mark had told her that she didn't attract him. When Lucas looked at her as though she had all the delights of paradise in her keeping past pain meant nothing; it slipped through her mind and away, like a bubble floating down a stream.

She said his name again, and drew in a ragged breath as he undid the buttons of her blouse. 'All right?' he asked.

She hated seeing the mask of control being reimposed. 'I'm not fragile,' she said, lifting her hand to undo his shirt.

He gave a short laugh, flicking back the silk revers, moving down her front. 'I think you are,' he said. 'But after tonight you won't have to worry ever again.'

'I'm not worried either.' She curled her hands around his face, holding him still. In a husky, slightly tremulous voice, she whispered, 'I trust you.'

'Thank God.' He looked down to where his fingers had reached the last button. Fragile silk fluttered in the soft puff of a vagrant breeze off the sea. He pushed the material off her shoulders and slipped his hand up behind her, undoing the catch of her bra with a single, swift movement.

'Take them off,' he said, his voice harsh in his throat.

Imprisoned and aroused by the primal energy vibrating through him, she slid her arms from the shirt and the bra, unzipped her trousers and let them drop to the ground. Beneath them she wore silk briefs, the palest, clearest pink, and she was more than repaid for the outrageous amount they had cost when she saw the look in Lucas's eyes.

'You have skin like satin,' he said thickly, wonderingly. 'Chaste white skin, until you blush and the colour trembles through it. You're like one of the old, proud, imperious goddesses, tall and full-breasted and full-hipped, taut-muscled, with an aura of danger and power about you. Men don't try to flirt with you, Anet, because you're dangerous; you're a risk to their ego.'

'But you flirted with me,' she pointed out, unbearably moved by his voice and his words.

'*No*. I saw you and I knew you. It was as simple as that.'

As indeed it had been for her. Simple and direct, yet she had been unable to see it for too long. And now it didn't matter; the world had closed down to this room in this house on this small island. No, her world was this man.

She reached out to help him with his clothes, her hands shaking as much as his. The fine tremor of his long fingers gave her a confidence she was sorely lacking.

But then everything about him gave her confidence: the light in his eyes when he looked at her, naked at last like a captive before her captor, her skin warm and tinted beneath the overpowering possessiveness in his gaze; the smile, humourless and set, that didn't soften his beautiful mouth when he touched her; the way his flesh was hot beneath her questing fingers; the smooth power of muscles and sinew contained by golden skin...

He loved her with tenderness and passion, tempering his great strength to hers, setting her aflame with a need so consuming she could only groan his name, gasp a plea for something she had never experienced. His skilful, questing fingers and clever mouth drove her remorselessly towards the end he was seeking, the sating of the hunger he roused. She moaned his name as she clutched at his shoulders, goaded by his fierce strength, aware of her own, intensely feminine power, at once demanding and submissive, giving and acceptant.

Only then, when his lovemaking had rendered her mindlessly lost in a dark and seductive tide, did he move over her and take her with one forceful thrust.

Sensation exulted through her. She took him in with a wild generosity, her hands exploring his back, feeling the taut, sleek muscles bunch and knot as he fought for control.

'Damn it, Lucas,' she muttered, 'don't you try to—' She moved her hips around him, drawing him deeper, using muscles honed by work and exercise to tip him over the edge.

'No—' he said, his voice deep and raw and guttural, but the particular brand of magic she had used on him wouldn't be gainsaid; he drove home with such sweet savagery that she gasped and crested, caught into another dimension where all that counted were the man whose

eyes were irradiated with love and need and ecstasy and
the incredible sensations he conjured from her body.

And then, when she could bear it no more, he joined
her in that realm, his face drawn with the agony of
rapture, the bonds of self temporarily suspended as they
lost themselves in each other.

Afterwards he locked her in his arms and said, 'Now
go to sleep.'

And she did.

She was unpacking the next morning when she saw the
little miniature. Somehow she wasn't surprised. 'You do
have a way of getting about,' she murmured, studying
the pictured face. Surely there couldn't be anything in
that poem? Had the miniature cast some sort of spell?

'No,' Lucas said calmly from the bed.

Her lashes flew up. He was looking at her with
amusement mixed with a flicker of anger.

'What?'

'I know exactly what you're thinking,' he said, leaning
over to take the painting from her hands. 'I didn't think
you were superstitious, Anet.'

'I'm not,' she said indignantly.

'So why are you wondering if she's some kind of love
charm? A dream can't be considered evidence. Anyway,
that's not what's worrying you, is it? You're wondering
whether she's cast a spell on me, so that what I feel for
you is false.'

Put like that, it sounded outrageously witless. She
mumbled, 'Not really.'

Dropping the precious little thing onto the table beside
the bed, he pulled her across until she was lying on top
of him, then hooked a finger under her chin so that her
face was exposed to his remorseless scrutiny. 'Not really?'
he asked silkily.

He was asking whether she believed that he loved her.
She sighed and said, 'I'm an idiot.'

'No, just still a little fragile. Try to believe, my dearest, my heart, that I wanted you when I saw you on
television, well before I ever saw you in the flesh, and
loved you as soon as I knew you. All that I have, all
that I can give, is yours. You hold my heart in your
hands, my life in your heart. I will love you until the
day I die. Nothing in this world or the next has the power
to change that.'

Tears brimmed into her eyes, magnifying the dark,
dilating pupils. 'I love you so much it terrifies me,' she
whispered. 'I'm sorry—perhaps one day I'll be able to
believe that you really are mine.'

'You will,' he promised deeply, his voice enormously
tender. 'Because I intend to reinforce it every day until
you do. I'm as much yours as you are mine. Totally,
deathlessly, without limits.' He kissed her, his hands
moulding her tightly to him so that she felt the swift,
electric anticipation race through him, leap to her own
body, charging every cell with consuming excitement.

'And when we get rid of the portrait, which we'll do
as soon as the right person comes along, you'll know
that I'm telling you the truth.'

'I know now,' Anet said, her voice drowsy with new-
wakened passion.

A trick of the light, perhaps the way the sunlight swayed
through the coconut fronds and fell aslant the little
portrait, made the painted face seem to smile.

* * * * *

*Look out next month for Jan Carruthers'
encounter with THE MARRIAGE MAKER in*
The Final Proposal.

HARLEQUIN PRESENTS®

The Marriage Maker
by
Robyn Donald

Can a picture from the past bring love to the present?

Coming next month:
the third and last story in
Robyn Donald's captivating new trilogy

#1877 THE FINAL PROPOSAL
Jan's Story

Available in April wherever
Harlequin books are sold.

HARLEQUIN 🕮 PRESENTS®

"A prolonged stay in my harem will provide me
with a long-awaited opportunity to teach you
what being a woman is all about."

Will Bethany pay the price that Crown Prince Razul
is demanding—and become his wife?

Watch for
#1875 THE DESERT BRIDE
by
Lynne Graham

Available wherever Harlequin books are sold.

Happy Birthday to

Harlequin Romance ®

It's party time....
This year is our
40th anniversary!

**Forty years of
bringing you the best
in romance fiction—and
the best just keeps
getting better!**

To celebrate, we're planning
three months of fun, and prizes.

Not to mention, of course,
some fabulous books...

The party starts in **April** with:

Betty Neels
Emma Richmond
Kate Denton
Barbara McMahon

Come join the party!

RANCH

Four generations of independent women...
Four heartwarming, romantic stories of the West...
Four incredible authors...

Fern Michaels
Jill Marie Landis
Dorsey Kelley
Chelley Kitzmiller

Saddle up with Heartbreak Ranch, an outstanding
Western collection that will take you on a whirlwind
trip through four generations and the exciting,
romantic adventures of four strong women who
have inherited the ranch from Bella Duprey,
famed Barbary Coast madam.

Available in March,
wherever Harlequin books are sold.

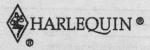

HARLEQUIN ®
®

HARLEQUIN®

Don't miss these Harlequin favorites by some of our most distinguished authors!
And now, you can receive a discount by ordering two or more titles!

HT#25645	THREE GROOMS AND A WIFE by JoAnn Ross	$3.25 U.S. $3.75 CAN.	☐
HT#25647	NOT THIS GUY by Glenda Sanders	$3.25 U.S. $3.75 CAN.	☐
HP#11725	THE WRONG KIND OF WIFE by Roberta Leigh	$3.25 U.S. $3.75 CAN.	☐
HP#11755	TIGER EYES by Robyn Donald	$3.25 U.S. $3.75 CAN.	☐
HR#03416	A WIFE IN WAITING by Jessica Steele	$3.25 U.S. $3.75 CAN.	☐
HR#03419	KIT AND THE COWBOY by Rebecca Winters	$3.25 U.S. $3.75 CAN.	☐
HS#70622	KIM & THE COWBOY by Margot Dalton	$3.50 U.S. $3.99 CAN.	☐
HS#70642	MONDAY'S CHILD by Janice Kaiser	$3.75 U.S. $4.25 CAN.	☐
HI#22342	BABY VS. THE BAR by M.J. Rodgers	$3.50 U.S. $3.99 CAN.	☐
HI#22382	SEE ME IN YOUR DREAMS by Patricia Rosemoor	$3.75 U.S. $4.25 CAN.	☐
HAR#16538	KISSED BY THE SEA by Rebecca Flanders	$3.50 U.S. $3.99 CAN.	☐
HAR#16603	MOMMY ON BOARD by Muriel Jensen	$3.50 U.S. $3.99 CAN.	☐
HH#28885	DESERT ROGUE by Erine Yorke	$4.50 U.S. $4.99 CAN.	☐
HH#28911	THE NORMAN'S HEART by Margaret Moore	$4.50 U.S. $4.99 CAN.	☐

(limited quantities available on certain titles)

	AMOUNT	$
DEDUCT:	**10% DISCOUNT FOR 2+ BOOKS**	$
ADD:	**POSTAGE & HANDLING** ($1.00 for one book, 50¢ for each additional)	$
	APPLICABLE TAXES*	$_____
	TOTAL PAYABLE	$_____
	(check or money order—please do not send cash)	

To order, complete this form and send it, along with a check or money order for the total above, payable to Harlequin Books, to: **In the U.S.:** 3010 Walden Avenue, P.O. Box 9047, Buffalo, NY 14269-9047; **In Canada:** P.O. Box 613, Fort Erie, Ontario, L2A 5X3.

Name:_____

Address:_____ City:_____

State/Prov.:_____ Zip/Postal Code:_____

*New York residents remit applicable sales taxes.
Canadian residents remit applicable GST and provincial taxes.
Look us up on-line at: http://www.romance.net

HBACK-JM4